'I don't know what burns between us, Mrs St Harlow, but there will come a time when we shall not have the will to stop it. I can promise you that.'

There—the words were said, falling against lies and covering them with a softer edge, like snow across the jagged sharpness of rocks.

The lump in her throat made her swallow as she tried to find an answer but what indeed could she say? If she agreed then only ruin would follow, and if she didn't…

She could not speak, even with everything held in the balance, and Lord Hawkhurst let her hand go and took a pace backwards.

AUTHOR NOTE

Three homeless and parentless boys are sent to Eton, where they forge a bond of friendship that can never be broken.

Now powerful lords, they need to marry, but the complex and intriguing women they choose mean that the road to happiness is not going to be an easy one.

Lucas Clairmont's story appeared in MISTLETOE MAGIC, Stephen Hawkhurst is the hero of MISTRESS AT MIDNIGHT and Nathaniel Lindsay's story will be coming next.

MISTRESS AT MIDNIGHT

Sophia James

First published in Great Britain 2013
by Mills & Boon, an imprint of Harlequin (UK) Limited.
Harlequin (UK) Limited, Eton House, 18-24 Paradise Road,
Richmond, Surrey TW9 1SR

ISBN: 978 0 263 89847 7

Harlequin (UK) policy is to use papers that are natural, renewable and recyclable products and made from wood grown in sustainable forests. The logging and manufacturing process conform to the legal environmental regulations of the country of origin.

Printed and bound in Spain
by Blackprint CPI, Barcelona

Sophia James lives in Chelsea Bay on Auckland, New Zealand's North Shore, with her husband, who is an artist. She has a degree in English and History from Auckland University and believes her love of writing was formed reading Georgette Heyer in the holidays at her grandmother's house.

Sophia enjoys getting feedback at www.sophiajames.net

Previous novels by the same author:

FALLEN ANGEL
ASHBLANE'S LADY
HIGH SEAS TO HIGH SOCIETY
MASQUERADING MISTRESS
KNIGHT OF GRACE
  (published as THE BORDER LORD in North America)
MISTLETOE MAGIC
  (part of *Christmas Betrothals*)
ONE UNASHAMED NIGHT
ONE ILLICIT NIGHT
CHRISTMAS AT BELHAVEN CASTLE
  (part of *Gift-Wrapped Governesses*)
LADY WITH THE DEVIL'S SCAR
THE DISSOLUTE DUKE

This one's for you, Nina.
I really appreciate your support.

Chapter One

June 1855—England

Stephen Hawkhurst, Lord of Atherton, felt the wind rise up from the bottom of Taylor's Gap, salt on its edge. He frowned as he breathed in, a smooth wooden railing all that held him between this world and the next one.

So very easy to end it, to simply let go and fall into oblivion. Pushing harder, he felt the barrier give and a few stones, dislodged by the movement, hurled down the incline to disappear into nothingness.

'If you jump, you would need to land exactly between that rock and the cliff,' a voice said, one small gloved hand pointing downwards. 'If you veer to the left, you will be caught on those bushes, you see, and such a fall could leave you merely crippled. To the right is a better option as the shale would be more forgiving before it threw you over the edge into the sea. However, if you excel at the art of swimming...?' She stopped, the implication understood.

Stiffening, Hawk turned to see a woman standing near, a black veil hiding every feature of her face. Her clothes were heavy and practical. A lady of commerce, perhaps? Or the daughter of a merchant? God, what luck was there in that? Miles from anywhere and the voice of reason close by.

'I may, of course, merely be taking in the view.' The irritation in his words was unbecoming and he was a man who was seldom rude to women. But this one was far from cowed.

'One would generally look to the horizon if that was the case, sir. The sun is setting, you see, and it would be this vista your eyes would be drawn towards.'

'Then perhaps I am tired?'

'Fatigue would show itself in a leaning gait and great exertion would be seen in dust upon your boots.' Her head tipped down to look. Stephen imagined her satisfaction when she saw his shiny new black Hessians. He wished she would turn and leave, but she stood silent and waiting, breath even and unhurried.

Surveying the nearby paths, he realised that she was alone. Unusual for a lady not to be chaperoned. He wondered how she had got here and where she would go to next.

There was a hole in the thumb of her right-hand glove and an unbuffed nail was bitten to the quick. The hat she wore hid her hair completely, though an errant curl of vibrant red had escaped from its clutches and lay across the darkness of her clothes like rubies in a coal seam. Beneath the notes of a heavier perfume he smelt the light freshness of violets.

'I came here often as a young girl with my mother and she would stand just where I am and speak of what was over the seas in all the directions that I might name.' This was said suddenly after a good few moments of silence. He liked how she did not feel the need to fill in every space with chatter. 'France lies that way, and Denmark, there. A thousand miles to the north-east a boat could

founder against the rocky coast of the King-
dom of Norway.'

She had a slight accent, though the cadence held the timbre of something that
Hawk did not recognise. The thought amused
him for he was a master of discerning that
which people wished not to divulge. He had
made his life from it, after all.

'Where is your mother now?'

'Oh, she left England many years ago. She
was French, you understand, and my father
had no desire to stop her in her travels.'

His interest was firmly caught as he took a
step back. 'He did not accompany her, then?'

'Papa loves poetry and text. His vocation
is as small as my mother's was large and
a library filled with books was all he ever
claimed to want in adventure. Her journeys
would have worried him.'

'The adventurer and the academic? An
interesting combination. Which parent do
you favour?' The question came from nowhere, for Stephen had certainly not meant
to voice it, but the woman had a charm that
was…unexpected. It had been a long time
since he had felt the sense of aliveness he
did here with her.

One hand crossed to her face, pushing the

gauze closer to her cheek. In the slanting light of sunset he could make out a finely chiselled nose. 'Neither,' she answered. 'The will to do exactly as one wants requires a certain amount of spare time which is a commodity I can ill afford.'

'Because you spend the day rearranging your father's extensive library?' He found himself smiling.

'Everyone has a story, sir, though your assumptions lack as much in truth as any tale that I might fashion around you.'

Stepping back another pace, he felt the bush at his back, sturdy and green. 'What would you say of me?'

'I would say that you are a man who leads others, though few really know you.'

Such a truth cut quick, because she was right. He seldom showed anyone who he was.

But she was not finished. Taking his hand, she turned it palm upwards, tracing the lines with her first finger. Stephen felt like snatching it back, away from the things that she might or might not see.

'You have a high falsetto singing voice, seldom touch strong drink and never bet at the New Year races at Newmarket.'

Her voice held a note of humour, and relief bloomed. 'So very exact. You ought to have a stall outside the Leadenhall.'

'It's a gift, sir,' she returned, her head tipping to one side as though measuring all that he was. Like a naturalist might watch an insect before sticking it through with a pin. There was something in her stillness that was unnerving and he tried his hardest to discern the rest of her features.

'Do you have a name?' Suddenly he wanted to know just who she was and where she came from. Coincidences were seldom as they seemed. His job had at least taught him that.

'Aurelia, my lord,' she offered, a new tone in his given title, a tone he understood too well. She gave no surname.

'You know who I am, then?'

'I have heard of you from many different people.'

'And the gossip of strangers is so very truthful.'

'It is my experience that beneath the embellishment, tittle-tattle always holds a measure of truth. It is said that you spend a lot of time away from England and its society?'

'I am easily bored.'

'Oh, I doubt that entirely.'

'And easily disappointed.'

'An explanation that may account for your presence here at Taylor's Gap.'

He breathed out hard, the possibility of blackmail creeping in unbidden.

She faced him directly, now, and lifted her veil. Freckles across the bridge of a fine nose were the first things he registered. Then he saw that one eye was blue and the other dark brown. A mismatched angel!

'It was an accident. A bleed. I fell from a horse as a child and hit my head hard.' This explanation was given in the tone of one who might have often said it.

She was so pale the blood in her veins could be seen through the skin at her temple. Like the wings of a butterfly, barely there. He wanted to lean forwards and touch such delicacy, but he did not because something in her eyes stopped him. He knew this familiar look of supplication, his many estates holding the promise of a largesse that was tantalising.

But not from her. The disappointment of it pierced hard even as she began to speak.

'I would ask a favour of you, Lord Hawkhurst.'

There. It was said, and in the circumstances he would have to be generous. It wasn't everyone who had seen the demons in him so clearly.

'Indeed.'

'I have a sister, Leonora Beauchamp, who is both young and beautiful and I want her to marry a man who would care for her well.'

As her words settled, fury solidified. 'I am not in the market for a wife, madam, no matter what you might like to say of this encounter.'

Her voice shook as she continued to speak. 'It isn't marriage I petition. I merely want you to invite Leonora to the ball I know you to be giving next week at your town house. I shall accompany her to ensure you know who it is to make some fuss of. A dance should do it, or two, if you will. After that I promise to never darken your pathway again.'

The anger in him abated slightly. 'To where should I send the invitations?'

'Braeburn House in Upper Brook Street. Any delivery boy would know of it.'

'How old is your sister?'

'Eighteen.'

'And you?'

She did not answer and his heart felt heavy as he looked down at her. 'So you are Aurelia Beauchamp?'

The shake of her head surprised him. 'Nay, that is Leonora's surname, but if you could see it in yourself to welcome my sister despite any…misgivings, I would be most appreciative.' Removing one glove, she delved into her pocket and brought out a pendant fashioned with a single diamond in white gold. 'I do not ask you to do this for nothing, Lord Hawkhurst, but if you say yes to the bargain between us I do expect you to hold up your end of it, without excuse. Could you promise me that?'

Interest began to creep under wrath, the flush on her face as becoming as any he had ever seen on a woman. She was a beauty! Beneath the fabric of her other hand he saw a ring, bold against the sheen of superfine.

Was she married? If she was his woman, he would have not let her roam the countryside so unprotected.

He smiled at such thoughts. Unprotected? Lord, was he finally growing a conscience? Thirty-one years old and all of them hard edged. The ends of his fingers curled against his thighs and he made himself breathe in, the souls of those he had sent to the afterlife calling close.

For Queen and for country or for the dubious needs of men left in charge of a foreign policy decades out of tune. Aye, England had not thanked him at all and he did not wish it to. But sometimes in a quiet corner of the world such as this one, and in the company of a woman who was as beautiful as she was beguiling, he wished for…something else.

He could not name it. It was too removed from the roads that he had followed, at first in wanderlust and excitement and now out of habit and ennui.

Murder, even in the circumstances of national security, sounded wrong. His father would have told him that, and his mother, too, had she lived. But they were long gone and the only family member left to give some guidance was Alfred; his uncle's scrambled mind still lurked in the remnants of the second Peninsular Campaign under Wellington, reality lost in the scarred remains of his left temple.

Stephen would have sworn had he been alone, but the sunset crept over her upturned face, painting untarnished skin the blush pink of dusk. The very sight of her took his

breath away. Like an angel offering redemption to a sinner, her fragile stillness warming
a heart long since encased in ice.

'Keep the pendant, madam, for I should
wish another payment altogether, here in
the open air and far from any community.'
The beat of his rising want hummed beneath
the banter. Part of him knew he should not
voice a request that was as inappropriate as it
was banal, but the larger part of him ignored
such a warning. He was a man who had lived
for years in the land of shadows and ill repute and it had rubbed off on him, he supposed. Aye, he almost welcomed the distance
scandal had brought, though sometimes, like
now, a crack appeared, small and fragile,
and a worm of longing for the good life that
he might have lived wriggled through. He
should turn and walk away, protecting the
little decency still left inside him.

But he didn't.

Instead he said that which had been building from the first moment of meeting her.
'All I want as payment is a kiss, given freely
and without anger.'

She waved such a notion away, the diamond clutched awkwardly in her hand. 'You
do not understand, my lord, it is my sister

whom I need you to introduce into polite society. It is not a liaison for myself that I seek here....'

'Then I refuse your terms.'

She was silent and still, long slender fingers worrying the dark folds of her skirt, and further away the birds gathered for a last chorus before slumber.

'Only a kiss, you say?' Whispered. Unbelieving.

The deep blush of blood bloomed under paleness.

He would know her name soon enough and then he would despise her as everybody else did, and too late to change it. But a chance for Leonora to be in the top echelons of London's Society was not to be dallied with.

One chance.

Fate had a way of occasionally throwing a lifeline and who was she to refuse? Even had he asked for more she could not have said no. For Leonora and for the twins. The stakes had risen as their circumstances had declined and with Papa... She shook her head. She would not think of him.

Goodness, why did he not just take the

pendant and be done with it? It was worth so much more than this nonsense he sought. And how was this to work? Did she face him and wait or did he require some prior flirtation?

A refusal would egg a man like him on. She knew it. Better to be sensible and allow him this one small favour, hold her lips up to his and close her eyes, tightly, until it was over.

His finger against her throat stopped every logical train of thought, the gentle play of the sensual so very unexpected. If she had been stronger, she might have stepped back and away. But the sensation of a man whose very name incited hysteria and frenzy amongst a great portion of the fairer sex in England caressing her was mesmerising and she could neither move nor call a stop to it.

The braiding holding the material of her gown together was thick and stiff, a resilient barrier to any more intimate caress. She was glad of such armour.

The hat surprised her, though, his free hand simply lifting the contraption off her head and away, the trailing ties lost in a growing wind as the piece fell to her feet.

'The colour of fire,' he said of her hair.

Or of shame, she thought, deep amber catching the final burst of sunset. She could see in his expression just what she had so often seen in those of others.

Uncertainty.

All the difficulties in her life surfaced, roaming free in her head, and she shut her eyes.

'Nay. I want you to see me.' He waited until she complied.

Closer he came, breath against her skin, the dark green of his pupils surrounded by gold. She could have fallen into those eyes, like the sky into a puddle, fathomlessly deep. Disorientated, she felt him draw her inwards, the muscles in his arms strong. She would remember this particular moment all the days of her life, she thought, with a heat of anticipation beating inside. His right temple held a raised crescent scar beneath the line of hair.

Blood surged through fear, like a river breaking its banks and running unconfined across a land it did not normally traverse, taking with it all that was more usually there. A changing landscape. An altered truth.

His heat was surprising. Each part of her skin seemed on fire as his lips took her own, ignoring the small token she thought to give him and opening her mouth to his tongue instead.

Inside, tasting, hard pressure and thin pain winding upwards from the depths of her being. Her fingers came to his neck of their own accord, threading through dark strands, her body splayed along the length of his, no space to separate them. She felt him turn her into a deeper embrace, the ache of need blooming over any sense that she might have tried to keep hold of, and she opened to him further. Her whole body now, legs jammed against the junction of his thighs, riding lust. His breathing was as hoarse as hers, no control, the huge yawning space of nature about them consigned to only this touch.

Hers. She wanted more. She wanted what she read of and dreamed about in her bed late at night as all the house slumbered and the banked fires dimmed.

She felt his masculinity through the wool of her skirt as he tipped his head to break the kiss.

'God.' The sound he uttered was neither soft nor gladdened. It was harsh and angry and uncertain, his mouth nuzzling her throat, biting into flesh, asking for completion, the knowledge of all he sought unspoken. When his thumb ran across the hardness of her nipple, flicking at the covering of bombazine, she simply went to pieces, the control that she had kept so tightly bound dissolving into disorder.

He held her against the half-light and the silence and the empty landscape, and release left her shaking. No sense in it, save feeling. When he raised her chin she took in the glory as he watched her, waves of passion wrenching gasps without voice. Lost and found, the gold in his eyes the only touchstone to a different reality, the tightened cords of lust entwined into every sinew of her body, her nails running unnoticed down the skin at his neck. A thousand hours or a single moment? She could not know the extent of her loss of governance until the world reformed and they were standing again on the top of Taylor's Gap.

Aurelia felt embarrassment and then shame. If he let her go, she would fall, like a boneless thing, all stamina gone. Laying her head against his chest, she listened to his heartbeat, the strong and even rhythm bringing her back.

'Thank you.' She could not say more and

to say less would have been mean spirited. He had to know that, at least, but in the face of her appalling behaviour all she wanted was to be gone.

Lord. She had come as he watched her, the feel of her body tight against his own and wonder in her eyes. Like quicksilver. Like magic. Like all his dreams wrapped into one, her long red hair curling against his skin, the serpent snakes of Medusa.

He knew not one single thing about her save that of a connection in flesh.

But he wanted her. He wanted to lay her down beneath the bushes behind them and remove the black and dowdy robe. He wanted to see her slender pale limbs in the oncoming moonlight as his hands wandered the lines of them before slipping into the wet warmth of her centre. He wanted to take her and know her again and again until there was nothing left of self, melded into the eternal.

His cock grew at such awareness and he could not stop the swelling.

She felt it, too. He saw the flicker of the awareness of danger in her eyes as her tongue took the dryness from her lips. He heard her breath quicken, the line of darker blue around one pale eye pulsating.

His woman. To take. The smell of her filled his nostrils, dangerous yet tempting, all the rules of gentlemanly conduct crossing over into darkness.

'Go.' It was all he could say for he did not trust himself enough to deny such want. 'I shall send you the invitations.'

The anger beneath his words must have registered because she moved back, shadow falling across her face, her hair lifting in the breeze as she turned, footsteps and then silence, only whorls of dust left in her wake.

Kneeling at the bottom of the railing, Stephen hung on to the solid wood, wild despondency all that was left. Lord, it was getting worse, this dispiritedness, claiming the early evening hours as well as the midnight ones. The demons of his past were gathering, armies of lost souls and foundered causes hammering at all he had stood for in the pursuit of justice. Could it have been for nothing?

Crumpling the black hat she had left behind in his fist, he looked for the brandy flask in his jacket pocket and undid the silver chain. Drinking deeply, he knew without a doubt that the solace of strong liquor was the only thing still keeping him sane.

The carriage she had rented was waiting in the place she had left it and she scrambled in, ordering the driver on even before she settled.

Away. Gone. It was all she wanted.

She should not have come to this place at all, but the memory of her mother here was strong and today, travelling between the mills and London, she had wanted to stop and remember.

Sylvienne had brought her here often because she said it reminded her of a place in Provence and for just a little while Mama did not stand in England, but in France, the mistral on her face and the little Alpilles at her back.

Aurelia would wait there with her, fingers laced together as her mother listened to the silence, her particular melancholy still remembered so vividly. Afterwards they would retire to one of the nearby villages for a drink and a meal and Mama would talk of her childhood, the heated sun and the trees that shaded roads bound by fields full of flowers.

And now here was another memory. Aurelia had recognised Lord Hawkhurst the moment she had seen him there, in the wind above the cliffs, his black cloak billowing and drawing her on despite misgivings. Had she gained a favour or lost one, she wondered, with her ridiculous reaction to his kiss? Shame had her breathing out hard and chastising herself for her inappropriate exchange with Lord Stephen Hawkhurst.

She should have insisted on the pendant as payment, but for a moment she had desired another truth, wanting to know something of unexpected passion and the melding together of souls.

She smiled wryly. Well, she had found that out. Bringing her hand to her lips, she touched her fingers to the place where they had been joined, trying to feel again the euphoria and delight.

Unexpected and addictive.

The sort of reaction her mother had made an art form of with her years of numerous lovers, reaching for that elusive and fleeting moment of forgetfulness.

A frown formed on Aurelia's brow.

She could not be the same, could not encourage feelings long since bottled to spring into a sort of half life, contained between scandal and ecstasy.

Which parent do you favour?

Five moments ago she would have answered 'Papa' without question, but now…?

No. The genie must be stopped before more emotions wanted to escape. She had learnt already the high price of her own ill-considered choices and now there were others needing her, depending on her…

Taking a deep breath she smoothed down her skirts and pulled her gloves on. She was an expert in the appearance of control; the smile of casual indifference she had perfected returned and the racing beat in her heart returned to quiet.

Lord Stephen Hawkhurst was to be avoided at all costs. His cousin had at least taught her that.

Chapter Two

London

'She's a lovely girl from a good family, Hawk. Safe. Pretty. Well thought of.'

There was something in the way Lucas Clairmont listed the attributes of Lady Elizabeth Berkeley that made him feel uneasy.

'You said you needed to settle down, for God's sake, and that you wanted to be a thousand miles away from the intrigues of Europe. As the only daughter of a respectable and aristocratic family, she certainly fits that bill.'

Finishing the drink he was holding, Stephen poured himself another before phrasing a question that had been worrying him.

'When you met Lillian, Luc, how did she make you feel?'

'My wife knocked me sideways. She took the ground from underneath my feet in the first glance and I hated her for it, whilst wanting her as I had never wanted another woman in my life.'

'I see.' The heart fell out of his argument. 'Elizabeth is more like a gentle wind or a quiet presence. When I kissed her once upon the hand she felt like a glass doll, ready to shatter into pieces should I take it further.'

Silence greeted this confession. Damn, Stephen thought, he should have said nothing, should have kept his mouth shut so that uncertainty did not escape to make him question an amiable and advantageous union. He was no longer young and Elizabeth Berkeley was the closest to coming near to what he thought he needed in a woman.

'There are different kinds of attractions, I suppose,' Luc finally replied. 'You seemed happy enough with the arrangements last week. What's changed that?'

'Nothing.' The room closed in on Hawk as he thought of his encounter at Taylor's Gap, fiery silk running through his fingers like living flame.

Elizabeth did not question him. She accepted all that he had been with a gentle grace. She saw only the goodness in people, their conviviality and well-mannered ways—a paragon of docility and charm.

Unease made him dizzy, the black holes of his life filling with empty nothingness. What might a woman such as that see inside him when the shutters fell away? Nay, he would never allow them to.

'I have it on good authority that her family expect you to offer for her. If you have any doubts…?'

'I do not.'

Damn it, he liked Elizabeth. He liked her composure and her contentment. He liked her dimples, her sunny nature and her pale blue eyes that were always smiling. He needed peace and serenity and she would give him this, a sop against the chaos that had begun to consume him. He filled up his third glass.

'You drink more than you ever have done, Hawk. Nat is as worried about you as I am.'

Smiling, the stretch of pretence felt tight around the edges of his mouth. Lucas Clairmont and Nathaniel Lindsay had been his best friends since childhood and each had had their demons.

'I remember saying the same to you not so long ago.'

'If you want to talk about it…'

'There is nothing to say. I am about to be betrothed to a woman who is as beautiful as she is good natured. I like her family and I like her disposition. She will give me heirs and I in turn will give her the security of the Atherton wealth and title.'

'Then it sounds like a sterling arrangement for you both. A marriage of much convenience.' The hollow ring of censure worried him.

'I am tired, Luc, tired of all that I have been. "A sterling arrangement", as you put it, might not be such a bad thing. Hemmed in by domesticity, I shall be happy.'

He picked at the superfine of his breeches as he spoke and crossed his legs. His boots reflected the chandelier, its many tiers of light spilling down into the room, everything bright upon the surface.

'Alexander Shavvon said you are doing more than reading codes for the Home Office?'

'Shavvon could never keep his mouth shut.'

'Ten years is too long to endure in service. Nat did five and nearly lost his soul. He swears that death stains everyone in the end whether they think it does or not.' The condemnation in his friend's words wasn't gentle, though Hawk knew the warning was given with the very best of intentions.

I kill people, Stephen thought as he opened his hand to the light. It shook now, all of the time, the tremors of memory translated into the flesh. *I take policy and make it personal again and again in the dark corruption of power. The black of night, the flame edge of gunpowder and the red crawl of blood. Those are my colours now.*

He wanted to tell Luc this, as a purge or as an atonement, but the words buried in secrecy would not form; the consequence of a life depending on camouflage, he supposed, and ceased to try to find an explanation.

Shadows, veils and mirrors. He could barely recognise the man he had become. Certainly, he did not defend the Realm with the cloak of justice firmly fixed across his shoulders any more; a score of innocent lives had seen to that particular loss as well as a hundred others who had no notion of such a word.

Aye, he needed the fresh, uncomplicated innocence of Elizabeth Berkeley like a man lost in the desert needed water.

'I am fine, Luc. I have a party about to begin in less than an hour and the promise of the company of a group of people around me whom I enjoy.'

'A happy man, then?'

'Indeed.'

Lucas nodded and leant forwards, his glass balanced on his knee. 'Lilly wants you at Fairley for Hope's twelfth birthday celebration. She says for me to tell you that were she not quite so pregnant she would be down herself to oversee your choice of a wife.'

Luc's words relaxed the tension markedly as both laughed, and when the clock at the end of the room boomed out the hour of eight they stood.

'Let the night begin,' Lucas said as Stephen finished what was left of his brandy and his man knocked on the door to tell them the first of the evening's guests would be arriving imminently.

Elizabeth Berkeley and her parents came in the second wave of company. Lady Berkeley looked like an older version of her off-spring and for a moment Stephen could see just exactly how her daughter would age: the small lines around her mouth, the droop of skin above her eyes, the social ease with which she sailed into any occasion.

His glance went to Elizabeth dressed in lemon silk and lace. 'It is so lovely to be here, my lord,' she said in a lilting whisper, placing one hand on his arm. Her nails were long and polished to a sheen.

A sudden flash of other fingers with nails bitten almost to the quick worried him, for he still wore their trails down his neck, hidden carefully under the folds of collar and tie.

Shaking away memory, he settled back into the moment as the Berkeleys moved on in the line of greeting and the next visitors came forth to be welcomed.

She was suddenly there beside him, the very last of the evening's guests, her hair wound up in an unflattering fashion, the black bombazine gown she wore unembellished and prim.

'Mrs Aurelia St Harlow and her sister Miss Leonora Beauchamp.'

A wave of hush covered the room at the

name, all eyes turning to the staircase. Aurelia was Charles St Harlow's widow? God, but she was brave.

'How on earth could she even think to come out in society, still?'

'It was she who killed him, of course.'

'Has the strumpet no shame at all?'

Threads of conversation reached Hawk even as she gave him her hand.

'I thank you for the kind invitation, my lord,' she said, her glance nowhere near meeting his own, 'and would like to introduce to you my sister Miss Leonora Beauchamp.'

The chit was charming, young and well mannered, but Hawk smiled only cursorily before turning back to the other.

'St Harlow was my cousin.'

For the first time, she looked at him directly, her eyes red rimmed from lack of sleep or from poorly placed cosmetics, he could not tell. She wore glasses that were so thick they distorted the shape of her face.

'We are almost family, then.' The smile accompanying the statement was hard.

He thought the sister might have turned away, but Aurelia held her there before him, her force of will biting through the atmosphere in the room, a small island of challenge and defiance.

Finally she leaned forwards and whispered, 'I gave you the exacted payment for the promise of this evening, my lord, and Leonora is not at fault here. Two dances and we will leave.'

'I am not sure, Lia. Perhaps we should go now.' The beginning of tears shone in the younger girl's frightened eyes.

'Do not cry, Leonora. It is me whom they despise. They will love you if you only let them.' Turning back, Stephen saw that Aurelia's hand shook before she buried it into the matt blackness of the wool in her skirt, but she did not give an inch. He had to admire such a resolute feistiness.

'If one beards the lion in his den, one must be brave.' Hawk related this to Miss Leonora Beauchamp and was glad when she smiled because the relief in Aurelia St Harlow's eyes was fathomless, hollow pools of mismatched colour focused upon him.

Years of deception flooded in. An unashamed façade undermined the certainty of others. If Aurelia St Harlow could brazen it out for an hour or more here, he doubted the rumours swirling around her would be quite as damning.

Lord. The promise of a dance with the sister had placed him in a position of difficulty, too. Charles had been one of the last living Hawkhursts, and the closest in blood to him save his uncle, but he had barely known him.

He saw Elizabeth with her family watching, her lips pinched in that particular way she had of showing worry. Guileless. He saw Luc observing him, too, the frown of anger on his brow as pronounced as those of many others. But even this could not make him withdraw his promise and order them gone.

His uncle next to him solved the whole thing entirely as he reached out and took the hand of the one woman in the world he should not have.

'I remember you, Mrs St Harlow. You are Charles's wife.' The use of the present tense made those within hearing press forwards. It was Hawk's experience that no one loved a scandal played out publicly more than the *ton*. 'I liked you right from the start, you see, but you got sadder. She needs to smile more, Stephen. Ask her to dance with you.'

Tragedy, farce and comedy now. The orchestra positioned only a few yards away from them looked at Hawk with expectation on hearing his uncle's loud command and the faces of those below were a mixture of indignation and shock.

He could do nothing less than consign Miss Leonora Beauchamp into the capable and kind hands of Cassandra Lindsay and offer Aurelia St Harlow the chance of a waltz.

The dance of love, he thought as he led her to the floor, and wondered why such a notion did not seem as ridiculous as he knew it should have. He hoped his right leg would stand up to the exercise, for of late the old wound had been playing up again.

When he placed his hands about her he felt her stiffen. 'It is my sister whom I would prefer to be where I stand, my lord, for if you adhere to the promised two dances I have just wasted half of them.'

He could not help but smile at such a comment. In response he tightened his grip and felt the full front of her generous bosom. When he looked down he saw she squinted behind thick spectacles.

'Glasses are supposed to cure poor eyesight, Mrs St Harlow, not cause it,' he said softly.

'Things to hide behind have their uses, however, my lord.' He noticed her straining away and gave her the distance because just the feel of her in his arms had begun to make his blood beat thicker. Across the room Elizabeth Berkeley and her parents followed them intently. 'You see, at a soirée such as this one it is preferable to be virtually invisible to those who might wish me ill.'

'They wish you ill because your husband's death was not one that made any sense. The fact that you were the only person there when it happened made you...culpable.'

'A court of law proved I had no hand in anything untoward, my lord. It is not my problem that the *ton* at large refuses to believe these documented facts.'

'Charles was an expert horseman.'

'Who fell at a hedge.'

'One does not generally end up with a sharpened stake embedded through the heart after such an encounter.'

'I am not here to argue my husband's unfortunate and early demise with you, my lord.'

The lack of any true feeling made Hawk pause, though his anger was softened a little when he felt the rapidity of her heartbeat beneath his fingers. She was good at hiding things, he thought. A spy's trait, that.

'Then why exactly are you here?'

'I have three younger sisters with little chance of an advantageous alliance unless they are out and about in society. As you can guess from my reception here tonight, we seldom receive any invitations. I am trying to remedy such a difficulty.'

'So you stalk the peerage in the hope of finding them in compromising positions and then inveigle a card requesting your company at their next social gathering?'

She laughed unexpectedly, the sound running through his bones into the empty darkness of his heart, and the room around them fell away into the windy barrenness of Taylor's Gap.

Was she a sorceress with her bright red hair and her different eyes? Had she bewitched his cousin in the very same manner? He wished the music might end, allowing him the ease of escape, but the orchestra was in full flight with no chance of a quick finale and to order it otherwise would only incite comment.

Aurelia St Harlow continued as if he had not insulted her at all. 'I had no knowledge of you being at Taylor's Gap, Lord Hawk. It was on a whim that I walked in your direction to admire the view and by a trick of coincidence found you there.'

'Fortuitous, then?'

'You speak of our kiss?'

He could barely believe that she would mention such a thing here in the crowded room of the *ton* at play and looked to see that none close had heard her question.

'There are ears everywhere in a gathering such as this one, Mrs St Harlow, and it is prudent to protect a reputation.'

She shook her head and looked away. 'Oh, mine is lost completely already, my lord. I doubt anything else I do could lower it further.'

Again he smiled, the freedom inherent in such a thought enlivening. 'How old are you?' Said before he could think, said from the very depths of interest.

'Twenty-six. An old maid. A woman on the shelf of life and happy for it.' Her eyes strayed to a set of females of a similar age sitting against one wall. 'I used to pity them until I realised how very liberated they actually were.'

His fingers tightened about hers, gloved

tonight in a strange hue of grey. He wished he might have felt her skin beneath, the warmth of it and the smoothness.

'My uncle seems more than taken with you and that is saying something. He seldom has time for anyone in society.'

For the first time that evening, genuine warmth entered her eyes. 'I always liked him, too. He showed me around the gardens at the Atherton country seat once and I helped him collect the eggs from the henhouses.'

'Most people ridicule him.'

'Most people loathe me so perhaps the thread in common allows us communion.'

'I do not loathe you, Aurelia.'

She tripped as he said it and fell up against him, the red in her face climbing into beetroot, though the dance music chose that particular point to end and he shepherded her back to her sister.

Chapter Three

Aurelia's cheeks burnt molten and the anger in her rose. Hell and damnation, but she was doing exactly what she had promised herself she would not do. She was feeling again and the ache about her heart made her sick and disorientated.

Not here, she chastised herself, not here amongst the wolves and jackals of a group who would like to do nothing more than tear her to pieces. A plain and untitled girl did not get away with treating one of their own the way she had treated her husband, after all.

Biting down, she swallowed, the thick glass in her spectacles blurring the edges of the room and making her queasy. Leonora at least looked happy and the young man beside her was both personable and well presented. Perhaps this evening would not be such a total loss after all.

Lord Hawkhurst stood next to a beautiful woman, her face wreathed in kindness.

'Lady Cassandra Lindsay, may I introduce Mrs Aurelia St Harlow.'

Lady Cassandra did not falter as she put out her hand in welcome, the grasp of her fingers warm and lingering. Such unexpected amiability was surprising, for it was far more common to encounter only censure.

'It has been a long while since I remember Stephen conversing so fervently with a dance partner.'

'The music did not allow him the courtesy of bidding me farewell, I am afraid, my lady,' she returned. 'I am certain he was much relieved when he was able to escape, though he has promised my sister a dance.' She got this in because Lord Hawkhurst looked anything but happy on the other side of the small circle of people.

'Oh, I rather think her card is full already, Mrs St Harlow. My brother Rodney has pencilled in at least two waltzes.'

Leonora fussed prettily as Lady Lindsay

introduced her brother to Aurelia and a small bloom of hope lingered in the air.

Could it even possibly be this easy? When Aurelia looked across at Lord Hawkhurst she saw the gold shards in his eyes harden. He was the tallest man in the room and easily the most prepossessing. No wonder women fell over their feet to be near him. But there was something under the visage that he presented to this society that was…darker.

Glancing away, she made much of extracting a lace handkerchief from her reticule. Charles had had the same sort of darkness, and look where that had got her.

Her sister, on the other hand, had a broad smile on her face and was using her fan most agilely. Aurelia had never seen her so animated and hoped that this was not a bad thing. Did men like a woman to talk quite as much? Was it not too forward to tap a man on the arm in the way that she was doing? Lady Lindsay's brother did not look in the slightest bit offended so perhaps such behaviour was expected. The headache that had been forming all day raked at the sides of her temple because she doubted that they would ever be given such a chance as excellent as this one again. The thought of coming away without contacts was dispiriting.

'Mr Northrup enjoys riding, Lia. I said he should accompany us for a canter around the Park.' Her sister's eyes were wide with hope, the blue in them matching her gown.

'Perhaps he should be careful, then, not to jump hedges,' Hawkhurst drawled in reply, though Cassandra Lindsay merely swatted his arm with her fan.

'Take no notice of Hawk, Mrs St Harlow. Charles was always taking great chances to show off his jumping skills. I couldn't believe he had not broken his neck before he…' She petered off, her brow furrowing, and the man beside her, whom Lia did not as yet know, began to speak.

'Before he died in the same way that the legends abounding in Transylvania tell of?'

Vampires? He spoke of such? The conversation amongst this group of people seemed irreverent and quick witted. No taboos. No carefully untouched subjects, and after Charles's rigid lack if humour such wit was refreshing. They laughed a lot, too, she thought, though Lord Hawkhurst's smile came nowhere near his eyes.

'You must not mind Hawk and my husband Nathaniel at all, Mrs St Harlow. I know how very difficult Charles's death must have been for you and I am certain that Rodney would love the chance of being invited into the charming company of your sister for an afternoon's ride. Where do you reside here in London?'

'Braeburn House, Lady Lindsay, in Mayfair.' Leonora was quick with her directions and Aurelia could only applaud her sister's acumen at seizing the moment, but the thought of Hawkhurst paying a social call was worrying.

What would he see there that she had tried to hide? Would they expect to meet Papa? Was there a chance he might talk with those about the area and understand things that she had been so successful thus far in concealing from others?

She was so exhausted with trying to tie all the threads of her life together she could barely breathe. How quickly could it all unravel?

The arrival of a young blonde woman and an older one within the group changed the tone of what was spoken of as introductions were given.

'You look as beautiful as ever, Lady Berkeley,' Cassandra's husband said as he kissed the back of the woman's hand.

'You were always the flatterer, Lord Lindsay. Your mother was the same, God bless her soul.'

The chatter was convivial and familiar between the people who had grown up all of their lives inside the sheltered world of the *ton*. Were Stephen Hawkhurst and Elizabeth Berkeley a couple promised to each other? The thought made Aurelia's head throb harder and she knew that she did not fit in here. She watched as the younger Berkeley woman shyly laid her gloved fingers on Lord Hawkhurst's arm and asked him a question beneath her breath.

His reply was as softly given back, the girl's cheeks glowing as excitement filled her eyes. Elizabeth Berkeley was like the first flush of some exquisite English rose: all promise, sweetness and hope. Aurelia could not remember a time when she had ever been like that.

At five she had watched her mother pack her bags and disappear. At six she had been the unwanted stepdaughter of her father's new wife and at seventeen Charles St Harlow had entered her life, like a falling star burning brightly.

Another waltz was struck and Lord Hawkhurst and Elizabeth Berkeley excused themselves to take to the floor, his arm around the young woman's waist in a careful ownership, the height and colouring of each exactly complementing the other.

'Did you know Hawk well when you were married to his cousin, Mrs St Harlow?' The question was from Cassandra Lindsay, eyes full of curiosity as she moved to stand directly beside Aurelia.

'No, I never once met him. His uncle, however, was a friend.'

A smile lit up Lady Lindsay's entire face. 'Alfred is rather picky about who he accords friendship to. Take Elizabeth Berkeley, for instance. I doubt he realises she exists.'

'She is very beautiful.'

'And quite lovely with it, which is a relief beyond measure if Stephen should decide to offer for her.'

'Which he will?' Aurelia had not meant to ask the question, and from the sharp interest in green eyes knew she had made a mistake by doing so. She was glad of the barrier of thick glass.

'Lord Hawkhurst has never taken a wife and his estate is more than healthy, so it behoves him to provide heirs. How long were you married to Charles?'

'Three years, my lady.' The tone of her voice was flatter than it should have been but tonight, with Leonora's face alight with possibility and hope, Aurelia was finding it hard to feign her usual pretence.

Cassandra Lindsay's next words were therefore unexpected. 'We are having a house party at our country estate in Kent in early September. Would you and your sister like to join us for the weekend?'

Her heart began to beat a little faster, the rhythm of it imbued with an unfamiliar kind of joy. It had been so long since a stranger had reached out a hand in friendship. Still, she could not quite accept the gift without honesty.

'Perhaps Leonora could attend with a chaperon, Lady Lindsay. My presence may be detrimental to the success of your gathering, you see, for there are many stories about me—'

Cassandra Lindsay broke in. 'There are always rumours, Mrs St Harlow, and there are always detractors, but anyone whom Uncle

Alfred takes a shine to I would trust with my life.'

'Thank you.' The ache in her throat was surprising as she glanced around, the heavy frowns of others less intimidating after such a conversation.

As the music ended the party regrouped. Elizabeth Berkeley had joined her mother to one side of the room, chatting with a group of other young women all dressed in differing shades of yellow. Stephen Hawkhurst unexpectedly walked back to Aurelia's side.

'Are you promised for this set, Mrs St Harlow?'

His question came quietly and in response Aurelia showed him her dance card without a scribble upon it. 'I seldom garner partners, my lord,' she returned, 'and certainly never the same man twice.'

His mouth turned up as he observed the empty page, and with the gracious strains of Strauss from the orchestra at the head of the room Aurelia felt disorientated.

Something else lingered there, too, but she did not care to examine those feelings as his fingers lifted the battered spectacles from her nose and held them away for a moment.

'Is that better?'

The faces of those around them came into full focus. 'Disfavour is often easier to stomach when it is barely seen, my lord.'

'Many here have their own skeletons should one bother to dig deeper, Mrs St Harlow. Take heart, for you are not the only person in the room with a past.'

Aurelia glanced away as he replaced her looking glasses. Did he speak about himself?

His hair was draped long across the nape of a snowy, crisp white collar, strands of midnight reflecting blue, the sense of danger and menace that she associated with him heightened here.

Charles had been a man who had promised everything and delivered nothing, a liar and a cheat who used those in positions of less power ruthlessly. Stephen Hawkhurst appeared to be the very opposite. She could not imagine him striking fraudulent bargains or making empty promises.

As his uncle joined them, the old man's hand reached down to extract a large handkerchief to wipe his shining brow. Alfred Hawkhurst's eyes were more opaque than she remembered them to be and he had a wheeze that was concerning.

'They don't want me there, Stephen. They never do. I can feel it when I speak to people.' His thin voice shook—a man who had had enough of the lofty world surrounding him.

'I feel exactly the same, Lord Alfred,' Aurelia began as his nephew failed to speak, 'though I find that the wine is helping.' She took two glasses from a passing waiter and handed one to him. Alfred smiled and downed the lot before leaning forwards in a conspiratorial way.

'You were always a favourite, my dear, and I am glad that you do not seem so melancholy now. I used to worry for you when Charles was about.'

Embarrassment swept through Aurelia's whole body. A thousand lies and yet an old man, reportedly mad, had seen through the lot of them. Like her father had. Catching the golden glance of Lord Hawkhurst, she looked away.

She had changed. She had grown up. No one could ever make her so sad again. The silk of Leonora's dress swirled cornflower blue in the middle of the floor, the weave of silver within it catching the light.

Macclesfield silk. Her lifeblood.

'I am more than content, Lord Alfred.' And quite competent, too, she thought. Dancing, needlework, luncheons and music—the pursuits of a well-brought-up young lady had long ceased to be a part of her domain. She tried hard to smile. She fitted nowhere now, like Alfred, lost in the middle somehow, an eternal outsider, looking in but never belonging. Not even knowing how to.

Her fingers strayed to the pendant at her throat, clutching the single diamond until she saw Lord Hawkhurst's eye upon the piece. Why had she worn it? The kiss at Taylor's Gap hung in the air between them in the particular manner of something unfinished. She could see the shape of it in his eyes and in the way he stood, his shoulders rigid with the tension of memory.

'I have always loved jewellery.' Alfred's proclamation was welcomed for it broke the unease, his outstretched hand touching the piece. 'What would you wish to be paid for this, my dear? Is it for sale?'

Hawkhurst carefully moved him back. 'Mrs St Harlow holds the bauble in much esteem and would part with it only under the most extreme of circumstances, Alfred.'

'She told you of that?'

'Indeed she did.' Shadows moved across his face, the planes at his cheeks softer now, and her body recalled the feel of Lord Hawkhurst's skin beneath her fingers, warm and solid, lips slanting deep with the taste of safety.

Aurelia shook her head. Such dreams were not ones she could contemplate again. Besides, had not Cassandra Lindsay stressed the need of a suitable bride at Atherton?

The black bombazine covering her from neck to foot was synonymous with the sort of life she led. Secretive. Careful. Lonely. In bed well after midnight and up well before the dawn.

When Elizabeth Berkeley came back to the circle Aurelia excused herself and wound her way to the ladies' room, where she sat for a good three-quarters of an hour on a chair in the small salon, completely impervious to the stares of others who were also using the chamber.

Another twenty minutes and she could be gone.

Hawk felt Elizabeth's fingers entwined in the fabric of his sleeve. He wished he might have shaken her off and followed Aurelia St

Harlow to wherever it was she had gone at least half an hour ago, but appearances had to be maintained and he was always careful in this respect.

Cassie Lindsay watched him vigilantly, too, as she had done for months now, her eyes upon him filled with question. She had made it known that she had asked Mrs St Harlow and her sister to their country seat of St Auburn's in a few weeks' time and that the invitation had been accepted.

The evening was going exactly as Mrs St Harlow would have wished it to and yet now she had disappeared off into a crowd that detested her and was lost to sight.

Alfred had gone looking for her. Just that fact amazed him as his uncle seldom stayed for more than a few moments at any of these public gatherings and never inveigled himself into the lives of those he met here. And what did he damn well mean by referring to her melancholy?

'I just love the colours of the gowns and the music, don't you, my lord? Everyone says that yellow is quite the shade of things this season.' Under the candelabras, Elizabeth's cheekbones were striking.

'Then you are eminently in fashion,' he

returned, her gown the colour of sunbeams shimmering in the light. The black bombazine of Mrs St Harlow came to mind, for his cousin had been years dead already and it was far past time to throw off the shades of mourning. He wondered how her hair might look against emerald green or a deep translucent gold.

No. He needed innocence and a lack of complication, he must remember that, the artless push of purity scattering the oncoming darkness. Why, Aurelia St Harlow probably had as many demons inside her as he did.

'I went today into town with Mama and found a jewellery shop that I had not noticed before.'

Stephen smiled, imagining Elizabeth enjoying the wares.

'Mama said I should have purchased the blue sapphire necklace because it showed off the colour of my eyes, but I preferred the ruby because it caught the light so beautifully. Do you think I have made a wise choice, my lord?'

His glance passed across the bauble nestled at her neck, the intricate patterns of gold fussy in design.

'It suits you entirely.'

'There was a bracelet to match, as well.' The glance she gave him had a certain entreaty in it. Hawk knew he should enquire as to the name of the shop and the exactness of its location given the unsaid promises shimmering between them, but the words just would not come.

He saw Mrs St Harlow threading her way back into the room from the corner of his eye. She looked neither left nor right, though even from this distance he could see women and men turning away from her in a deliberate cut. Her chin rose and if he had not known of her unease in the social setting he might have thought that she did not care a jot for the good opinion of others. He was glad she had the glasses to shelter behind.

'Do you not think so, my lord?'

The pale beauty of Elizabeth's puzzled gaze fell upon him.

'I do.' He had no idea at all as to what he had just agreed but his attention was caught by a group of men Aurelia was about to walk past on one side of the room.

Lord Frederick Delsarte caught her arm, tightly, and held it. Stephen could see the others folding in about her, blocking off any means of escape. The smile she wore was imbued with solid anger, though even from this distance he could detect a certain panic.

'Would you excuse me for a moment, Miss Berkeley?'

He did not wait for any reply, but strode across to the colonnade shielding the group from the notice of others and walked straight into the contretemps.

'There you are, Mrs St Harlow,' he said, placing Aurelia's hand across the material of his sleeve as he pulled her into his side. 'Lady Lindsay is most anxious to find you. Something about meeting an old school friend, I think she said.'

Unfortunately Delsarte had had too much to drink and was in no mood to observe the social niceties. 'We have not finished here,' he slurred with difficulty, 'and your cousin's widow and I have much to talk about.'

'I sincerely doubt that, Delsarte.' Hawk hurst's free hand slipped to the top of the younger man's arm and pressed, the yowl of pain heartening.

'It's Hawkhurst, for God's sake, Freddy,' a taller man next to Delsarte whispered in the tone Stephen had become accustomed to people using around him.

'I would greatly prefer it if you were not

to venture anywhere near Mrs St Harlow again, do you understand?'

Caution finally shone through bloodshot eyes. 'I didn't realise you knew her so well, Lord Hawkhurst.'

'Ahhh, but now you do.' Hawk let go his hold and stepped back, shepherding Aurelia before him as they moved out from behind the pillars.

Fury raced through him as he saw the paleness of her skin welting already into bruises where the bombazine had ridden above her wrist in the struggle. He also saw she swallowed often as though trying to keep back the tears, but he could not be kind. 'Why the hell would you go off alone and unprotected when you know the communal feeling in the room is so against you? Surely you understand the dangers inherent in social animosity?'

She took a breath. 'Hatred is generally less demonstrative,' she returned, and had the temerity to smile.

Hawkhurst looked as if he wanted to kill her, here in the ballroom twenty yards from the woman it was said he would marry, and the ache in her arm from where Freddy

Delsarte had grabbed her was beginning to throb.

If Hawk had not intervened, she wondered what might have happened. Could they have dragged her from the room kicking and screaming and not a soul willing to lift a hand in aid?

Save for him.

She should not have come. It was too dangerous and too uncertain and Charles's more carnal predilections were shown within the leer of the younger man's eyes. She knew Hawk had seen this, too, for his grip upon her had tightened imperceptibly.

'You incite great emotion in those about you, Mrs St Harlow, even in the dress of a dowager.'

'Men see what they wish to see, my lord. It is a fault that is universal.'

'I cannot remember you much in the company of my cousin. It seemed you were never in London at all.'

Breathe, Aurelia instructed herself when she realised she had simply stopped doing so, the beat of her heart racing through the thickness of black wool.

'There was always much to do at Medlands. Gardening was one of my particular

favourites and Charles enjoyed the colours.'
She tried to imbue the sort of gladness that
she imagined a lady of leisure might feel for
such a hobby, her mind scrambling around
for the names of common plants just in case
he took the conversation further.

'Then you must have been saddened to
see the house sold on his death?'

Worry turned. As Charles's only cousin
he did not know? She could scarcely believe that he would not, although the fact
that Lord Hawkhurst was rumoured to have
barely been in England for many years made
it seem more than possible. Perhaps no one
save her lawyers knew of the financial col-
lapse that her husband had left her in, a hundred chits from the merchants of Medlands
village presented and little money to honour
them. She had been so careful to pay them
back, after all.

Medlands sheltered another family now
and Aurelia had not been sorry to pack up
the few belongings that were her own and
leave the place for ever.

'I have many memories left to remind
me, Lord Hawkhurst.' *Shame. Anger. Disappointment. Murder.*

He watched her carefully, the shadows in

his eyes pulled back into puzzlement. With him at her side she felt completely safe, the stares of those around her muted in his company. She wished he would ask her to dance again as the music of a waltz was struck but, of course, he did not as they came into the little group she had left a good fifty minutes earlier. The young and beautiful Elizabeth Berkeley was again quick to take his arm. Aurelia thought she would have liked to have done the same, simply laid her fingers across such security and held on.

She remembered Freddy Delsarte at the parties at Medlands come Christmas, where the girls from London were brought up to satisfy the wants of married men who had long become bored of their wives.

As Charles had with her.

Closing her eyes, a dizziness that had become more frequent of late made her world spin.

'Are you quite well, Mrs St Harlow? You suddenly seem very pale.' Cassandra Lindsay's tone was worried.

'Just tiredness, I think,' Aurelia returned, looking at Leonora and Cassandra's brother on the dance floor enjoying each other's company.

'I could bring your sister back, if you would like, and Stephen could organise a carriage to take you home immediately. We will not be late ourselves and I promise you I would chaperon her as if she were my own daughter.'

The offer was tempting with Charles's friends watching her from one corner and the rest of the *ton* scowling from the others.

'If it would not be too much trouble…?'

Cassandra Lindsay's smile was bright as she bid Aurelia goodnight. Then she drew Elizabeth Berkeley away from her grip on Lord Hawkhurst's person with talk of the colour and cut of the gowns that were her very favourite in the room tonight.

Aurelia gained the distinct impression that in doing so the woman was helping her.

Chapter Four

'I most certainly did not expect you to accompany me home, Lord Hawkhurst.'

He smiled, his teeth white in the dark of the carriage and his thighs less than an inch from her own. 'But I wanted to, Mrs St Harlow, because it will give us the chance to talk about how it is you know Lord Frederick Delsarte and his lackeys.'

'They were acquaintances of my husband.'

'But not of yours?' No humour lingered now, his voice cold, cut glass.

She shook her head. 'My disapproval of their antics was more than obvious, I should imagine.'

'Did Charles ever hurt you?'

The very intimacy of the question made

her turn away. 'No. He was a wonderful husband.' The words were exactly those she had used in the courts when the law had tried to lay the blame at her feet for his unexplained death.

'Why is it that I think you lie?'

She turned back. 'I have no idea, my lord.'

The air all around them contained something that she had never felt before. The pure and utter longing for a man, this man, their unfinished kiss from a week before shimmering on the edge of a lust so foreign it made her feel light headed.

'Charles enjoyed a wide interpretation of the word "fairness" and when he died at Medlands there were probably a number of people both in London and further afield who breathed a sigh of relief to hear of his passing. As his wife you must have known this.'

Such criticism hung in the darkness, a living and breathing thing, defining all that Charles had been. Given that what he said held a great dollop of truth Aurelia found it hard to argue. 'There were also a number who may have mourned him.' She stated this with as much certainty as she could feign. Those who came up for the party weekends at a country mansion who held strict morals in little worth probably rued his passing, but she doubted there were many others. The Medlands estate had buried him with a smile upon its collective face, their lord and master a man who held little regard for the feelings and needs of others more lowly born than he was.

When Lord Hawkhurst caught her hand and held it tight, she could feel tremors within the strength—a surprising thing, that, given his easy confidence. The night of London was black and endless, a quarter-moon lost behind banks of cloud, leaving only them in the dark and empty space of the world.

The warmth of his skin comforted her though, a solid contact amidst all that was strange and she felt her fingers curl around his. He did nothing to resist.

'I would have asked you to dance again if I knew a scandal wouldn't have ensued because of it.'

She could not believe he would admit this, to her, a stranger. 'Lady Elizabeth Berkeley may not have been pleased about that,' she retorted, hating the bait she threw at him. It was beneath her to involve such an innocent young beauty for her own means, but there it was and she did not take it back. Rather, she waited.

'A title like mine, and the possessions accompanying it, have a way of garnering interest. It is a known fact.'

'Such is the ease of being wealthy.'

'Charles was rich, too. Perhaps you are more like Elizabeth Berkeley than you think.'

She did laugh at that, the sound lost into a mirth that was humourless. 'I cannot determine one trait that we might share, my lord.'

'What of beauty?' he replied.

Was this a joke he played upon her? 'I am hardly that, my lord.'

'A woman who does not know her true worth is a rare and valuable thing.' His voice allowed no tremor of falsity and when she turned towards him the breath left her body, his expression exactly the one she had seen at Taylor's Gap: lust and want beaten back by will.

Breaking the contact, he fisted his palm against his thighs so that every knuckle stretched white. The scars on his knuckles stood out as raised edges of knotted flesh.

He swore soundly, the frustration expressed coursing between them. She should have bidden him to let her make the rest of the journey alone, should have replaced her gloves with a stern reprimand and ordered him from the carriage. But she could not. Instead she sat there, too, the silence growing as an ache, her hands bare in her lap and cold, her head heavy against the cushioned velour of the seat. For twenty-six long years she had imagined exactly this, a man who might transport her from the tight restraint of her life and deliver her into temptation.

His eyes glinted in the dark when she chanced to take a look, the bleakness in them shivering through green.

'Your husband had questionable friends, Aurelia. Take care that they do not become your own.'

He would warn her even given the public perception of her part in Charles's murder. Gratitude rose unbidden.

'I live a simple and quiet life with my father and sisters. There is little in me that could be of interest to anyone.'

His laugh was menacing. 'Somehow I doubt that entirely.' The residual feeling existing between them since their kiss thickened. What on earth was happening to her? Hope drove into a veiled anger.

He would never be hers. It was written in exactly who she was. As she moved away carefully, the space between them became bathed in a pool of light reaching in from outside and when she saw that they were back in Upper Brook Street the relief was indescribable.

Braeburn House. The horses slowed to an amble and then stopped as Aurelia stretched the fabric of her unworn gloves out whilst deciding exactly what it was she would say. There were so many things that she might have told him, but in the end she settled on the one that would keep her family safe.

'I relinquish you from any bargain that stands between us, my lord, and I realise that my insistence on an invitation to your ball was both forward and foolish.' She enunciated the words very carefully and hoped that the need in her was not as visible as she thought it might be.

'Your sister and Rodney Northrup may not say the same, Mrs St Harlow.'

The words were cold and stilted, none of the delight of the evening held within them, and as if to underline his desire to have her gone he simply leaned across to the door and flipped the handle, gesturing to one of his servants to help her alight.

He should not have been alone with her, jammed into the small space with the warmth of her skin and the rapid beat of her heart searing into all his good intentions. Aurelia St Harlow was his cousin's widow and he was all but promised to Elizabeth Berkeley.

The anger in him grew along with a more unfamiliar frustration as he ran his fingers across his face, hating the way he was never able to hold them still. The night had left him wrung out and tired with the wax and wane of emotion and he still had a great deal of it to get through before everybody left. He wished that the hour was later and that the throng who danced and laughed in the Hawkhurst town house could have been gone, especially the Berkeleys. He did not have the energy to deal with Elizabeth's unrelenting innocence in the light of his thoughts in the carriage, or the hopeful encouragement of her mother. He also knew that as the host he should not have left the party, but the opportunity for time alone with Aurelia St Harlow had been too enticing.

* * *

Cassandra Lindsay greeted him as he walked back into his downstairs salon a little time later.

'Lady Elizabeth has been asking after you, Hawk. I said that I had seen you in conversation with Lord Calthorp and that you were heading towards the library.'

Sometimes, Hawkhurst felt Cassie knew a lot more than she let on.

'Business,' he returned and took a drink from one of the passing waiters as Nat and Lucas joined them.

'The St Harlow widow is gone, then?' Luc asked. 'She looked nothing like the sort of wife I imagined Charles to take.'

'What had you imagined?' Nathaniel asked the question and Stephen was glad for it.

'Someone of less substance, perhaps.'

'Leonora Beauchamp spoke very highly of the sister, too,' Cassie put in. 'There are two other younger sisters, by her account, who will be out in the next few years.'

'And the father?' Stephen did not want to ask the question, but found himself doing so.

'Sir Richard Beauchamp. He keeps to himself and seldom ventures into town. He is known as somewhat of an eccentric academic, a man of few words and little animation. Mrs St Harlow drives him around the park on a Monday afternoon straight after the luncheon hour, but they rarely stop to socialise with anyone.'

'I get the feeling she is not quite the woman that society paints her to be.' Lucas's smile was puzzled.

'If she wore a dress that showed off something of her very fine figure and a style that enhanced the vivid red of her hair she could be an original. Where on earth do you think she got the black gown? It looked like something a dowager would have worn back in the Regency days.' Cassandra addressed the query to Hawkhurst, who shrugged it off as he watched his uncle thread his way through the room to join them.

'I cannot find her anywhere, Stephen. Mrs St Harlow is quite gone.'

'That is because I ordered a carriage to take her home, Alfred.'

'Your man said that you were in it, too.' Opaque eyes glinted in the sort of wily knowledge few understood his uncle to have retained. He was pleased Elizabeth was speaking with her mother a little way off, though he knew from the flare in Cassie's eyes that she would make much of the revelation when she was able. Both Nat and Luc displayed no trace of hearing anything.

A careful neglect, he surmised, and turned his attention back to Elizabeth Berkeley as she joined them.

'Your ball is becoming the very crush of the Season, my lord. I have never in all my life seen so many of the *ton* in one place and dancing.'

Stephen smiled, Elizabeth's bright and happy reflection making him relax. 'Lady Lindsay and Mrs Clairmont had a great deal of say in the organisation. Any success owes more to their management than my own.'

'Mama says that it is a rare man who can inveigle so many to attend in the first place, and the supper was magnificent. Why, there are people here I have not seen venture out to any other soirée all Season.'

'The power of a fortune is not to be easily underestimated, Lady Elizabeth.' Nat's tone was laconic.

'I said exactly the same to my friends, Lord Lindsay, and they were all in agreement.'

'Then I rest my case.'

Elizabeth's fluster made Hawkhurst want to laugh, her innocence no match for the cynicism of his friend, but he did not because in the admission of such naivety another quandary rose unbidden. Could he really live for ever in the shadow of such unimpeachable trust without wanting more? The quick burst of risk? The enlivening rush of a gamble?

Leonora Beauchamp swept by them in the arms of Rodney Northrup at that very moment, all blond curls and youthful exuberance, the waltz giving them an excuse for closeness that no other dance managed to.

'She is so very pretty,' Elizabeth's mother tapped her fan closed against her arm. 'It is a shame that she comes tarnished by the reputation of her oldest sibling. My husband says if she had sense, Mrs St Harlow would leave society altogether and never return.'

Truth. How skewered it could become. Aurelia had risked everything for her sister's welfare and none would ever know of it. He smiled, for 'leaving society altogether' might have been her most ardent wish.

A group of Elizabeth's friends now stood beside her. He could tell that they had heard the words uttered about his cousin's widow because the look of agreement and gossip was written full on their faces. Excusing himself summarily, he went to find a drink.

Aurelia sat in the downstairs salon near the hallway on a chair that was hard and straight, waiting for Leonora to come home. It was later than Lady Lindsay had promised it would be and she felt an exhaustion rise up that made her bone-weary. The clock at the other end of the room pointed to the hour of one, and she knew John, their servant, was waiting and then he, too, could find his repose.

He had left the lights burning this evening at her request, which was an expensive luxury, and they both watched the shadows at the window, listening for a noise. Finally it came.

'They are here, ma'am.'

Nodding, she watched as he took a lamp and went out to greet the carriage. The laughter and the voices were joyful, Leonora's particularly so, as she bid her companions goodnight.

A few moments later her sister was back inside and the large front door was closed against the darkness.

'I have never in all my life had such a

wonderful night,' she trilled, turning on the floor as though she was still dancing with an imaginary Rodney. 'Mr Northrup will come and call on us tomorrow, I am certain of it. Oh, Lia, you are the most caring sister in the whole world to have procured such an invitation for me.'

Her overt enthusiasm only had the effect of making Aurelia feel older and more tired and she was glad when Leonora bade them good evening and went to find the twins in their beds. To regale the whole episode to them, she supposed, and hoped that they would not wake Papa in their excitement.

John doused the flame of the lamp, his brow lined in worry.

'The young gentleman was adamant about shepherding Miss Leonora in until I told him that your father had been ill with the influenza, Miss Aurelia, but he seemed most anxious to visit.'

'Then let us hope he does not stay long.'

'I sometimes think, ma'am, that it is my family who has made everything impossible for you and that it would have been better had we just disappeared—'

She didn't let him finish. 'The court came to the conclusion that no one was to blame save Charles for his own death, John. It is my opinion that they were right.'

'Without your help they may have come to another decision altogether.' His face held the agony she had become accustomed to seeing there—an old man with the weight of secrets and sadness upon his shoulders. She recognised his anguish as the same emotion that crouched inside of her, waiting to pounce, biding its time.

'And any other decision would have been an erroneous one, given all the facts.'

The older servant bowed his head and nodded before going to check that the doors were fastened. He had aged considerably in the years since Charles had been dead, but then so had she, his influence still lingering long after his demise.

Of a sudden she felt light-headed and dizzy. She had not eaten anything at the Hawkhurst ball and had been too busy helping finish the last stitches in Leonora's gown to take succour at lunchtime, and here was a stranger who would be back knocking at the door of Braeburn House in only a matter of hours.

Had she made a huge mistake by petitioning Lord Hawkhurst for the invitations? She shook her head. No, there was nothing else she could have done and with careful management the whole thing could still work to their advantage for Leonora had been more than taken with Rodney Northrup.

It could have been a lot worse. Cassandra Lindsay's brother seemed a kind man and the influenza that John had mentioned was also inspired. No one would expect Papa to appear downstairs for a good week or two at least.

Looking around, she was pleased they had kept a hold of some of the better furniture, though there were places where more expensive artefacts had once languished. The missing pieces were her inheritance, mostly; she had been careful not to strip the house of those things Leonora, Harriet and Prudence held dear.

They were finally gone, the last of the guests on their way home at almost five in the morning. Hawkhurst imagined the first flush of dawn on the eastern horizon as he climbed the stairs to his bedroom on the first floor.

He had met his agent and exchanged the papers, easily and secretly. He had watched

Delsarte and his group, too, for there were rumours of an involvement in clandestine activities that the British Service wanted some measure of. Aurelia's contretemps with Delsarte came to mind, his mission of watching the lord and his minions suddenly at risk. The personal and the professional were beginning to impinge on each other and he knew he would need to be more careful. Ten years of stellar service to his country were not to be taken away on a…whim. Hawk frowned at the word as he lay down, kicking off his shoes and watching the play of light and shadow outside through his undrawn curtains.

'Aurelia St Harlow.' He whispered the name into the darkness, listening to the sound of it return to him like some forbidden music.

Elizabeth Berkeley was softer and more familiar, yet it was not to the blond ringlets and pale eyes that his mind wandered as he remembered his cousin's widow writhing against him in the dusk.

He wanted to kiss Aurelia and feel again what he had once, the sharp and unexpected delight of lust surprising him, for it had been many a year since he had known the sort of quickness that she inspired. The anger at such a demented fantasy had him sitting upright.

She was a woman who was said to have killed his cousin and got away with it, the whispered gossip of society following her every step. She would be forever ostracized and dismissed. He breathed out with a heavy force of air, for years of being a rolling stone had worn him away, homeless and searching, the shadows now thick harbingers of all he had become. He needed the security of a warm and easy home. He needed goodness and humanity and mercy to heal his demons, crouched now closer than ever. Taylor's Gap had been a warning of his precarious state of mind and he knew he had to be more careful for with only a little push he might lose the touchstones altogether.

He opened a drawer on a small cabinet beside his bed and took out a box. A golden timepiece lay inside. His brother's. Stopped at the moment of his death. The claws of grief had him standing and he made his way to the seat by the window to watch the heavens, a distant glimmer of light claiming the darkness to the east as dawn finally broke.

Alone. For so long now. The burden of

it all made worse by his need for an heir. He swore as the hallowed legends of the Hawkhurst family wrapped around his chest so tightly he found it hard to move. The scent of violets felt close and his leg ached in the early morning cold.

Chapter Five

'No, Papa, you have to eat your breakfast.'

Aurelia had had three hours' sleep last night and she swallowed down irritation as her father refused to open his mouth, her eyes straying to the clock on the mantel. Eight o'clock already. She hoped Mr Rodney Northrup would not come calling until well into the afternoon, although she could already hear Leonora preparing herself for his visit.

'I want to read, Lia. I want to sit and read.' His hand came out and she smiled when warm fingers curled into her own. It had been two years since the father they had known had been largely swallowed up by a stranger that they did not, but sometimes like now there were the old glimpses of him.

'Eat the egg, Papa, and then I will take you into the library.'

When he finally allowed her to feed him she breathed a sigh of relief. 'Leonora has a beau coming to see her this afternoon. His name is Mr Rodney Northrup and he is a friend of Lord Hawkhurst.' Aurelia always told him the news of the house each morning just in case he might take something in.

Prudence joined her after a few moments, her youngest sister's face alight with anticipation, her hair a golden froth of curls.

'Leonora says Rodney Northrup is the most handsome boy she has ever met, Lia. She says that he danced with her all night and sat close beside her in the carriage on the way home. She also mentioned that you had had a waltz with the menacing Lord Hawkhurst. Could you not have refused him?'

'Hawkhurst?' Her father spluttered the name. 'Charles knew Hawkhurst?'

'Indeed, Papa, he did.'

Prudence's eyes widened. 'Did Papa just understand us, Lia?'

Aurelia waited to see if her father would say more, but silence seemed to have claimed

him again as he sat and fiddled with a spoon
and a fork.

'There are glimmers of comprehension
still, Pru, although we have to expect that
they will become fewer and further between,
but enough of all this for now. Tell me, what
is Leonora wearing today?' The topic distracted her sister completely and as she
talked excitedly about a silk gown trimmed
with lace, Aurelia wandered her own pathway of thoughts.

Would Stephen Hawkhurst accompany
Rodney Northrup? She hoped that he would
not. *Please, God, let him not come,* she
prayed over and over, jolted from her mus-
ings as her sister asked a question.

'Did the invitation to Lady Lindsay's
country party include Harriet and me?'

'As you have not even come out yet I
should doubt it very much!'

'But we are almost seventeen, Lia. Could
we not at least plan a time when we should
be able to accompany you to such things?
We could borrow the older gowns Leonora
no longer fits. It won't be expensive.'

The plaintive tone in her voice had Aurelia taking a breath. When would it ever be

easy? The silks were beginning to pay, but their debts were still substantial.

She should be at the warehouse now, sorting through fabric, but this visit by Cassandra Lindsay's brother meant that she needed to be at home today, chaperoning her sisters as there was nobody else to do it.

As she closed her eyes the exhaustion she had felt last night was there again this morning so, after finishing her father's leftover breakfast, she poured herself a glass of milk. If she became ill then the whole game was lost. One mistake and her father's second cousin would be in to claim Braeburn House, leaving them homeless and penniless.

The horror of such a thing happening was not even to be considered and she stood to help her father back to the library. He did not understand what he read any more, but he enjoyed holding the books. She would instruct his maid to keep him there until after the visitors had gone, influenza giving her a good excuse for his absence.

Rodney Northrup was accompanied by his sister and they arrived well into the afternoon.

They were all in the downstairs salon

when they heard the sound of a carriage stopping. Prudence ran to the window to be roundly growled at by Leonora who wanted everything to be simply perfect. Harriet rolled her eyes at Aurelia as they all took their seats again and listened to the approaching voices.

He was not with them! Relief flooded into Aurelia's whole body. Hawkhurst had not come with his golden eyes, night-dark hair and menacing certainty. She unclenched her fists, removed her glasses and found herself smiling as Cassandra Lindsay and Rodney Northrup were shown into the room by John.

'I hope we did not keep you waiting at all.'

'You are right on time, Lady Lindsay,' Aurelia returned, her sentiment not echoed in the face of both Prudence and Harriet.

'Oh, please call me Cassie. All of my friends do.'

Without waiting for a reply she clasped Leonora's hands next. 'Rodney has been most keen to come today, my dear, and with you looking so pretty in pink I can well see why. Your two sisters mirror you in their pastel hues.' She waited as Aurelia introduced the twins, their curly blond hair catching the light from the window.

'I did not realise your sisters were almost all of the same age, Mrs St Harlow.'

'Prudence and Harriet are nearly seventeen. They will come out next Season.' Aurelia did not quite feel comfortable using Lady Lindsay's first name and so did not add anything else at all.

'And your father?'

'Is indisposed at the moment with the influenza. He is in bed and has been for the past few days.'

'Then let us hope he makes a good recovery with no lingering bad effects.'

In answer Aurelia smiled, the lies falling bald into the room between them. It had been so long since any stranger had set foot in Braeburn House and the need for lies made everything dangerous. Her eyes strayed to the clock. How long did one of these visits usually last for? She hoped it might be quick.

'I visited Mrs St Harlow and her sisters yesterday with Rodney, Hawk. Aurelia St Harlow is…unusual.'

Cassie's statement made both men turn from their seats in the corner of the St Auburn library.

'She wore the same dress we saw her in

at your ball, which was interesting, though she had done away with the glasses. Her eyes are the most surprising of colours. Different shades,' she continued as neither her husband nor Stephen spoke. 'I wonder why she hides herself beneath yards and yards of shapeless black bombazine.'

Nat began to smile. 'What are you trying to tell us, Cassie?'

'Secrets linger in Mrs St Harlow's eyes like ghosts and she is careful with every single thing that she says. Charles, of course, was difficult, so that may be part of it. But there are other things, as well. The same servant who greeted us at the carriage after the ball last night took our coats, provided us with tea and showed us out.'

'You think they are short of money?' Hawkhurst made the observation.

'The house is furnished well and is one of the prettiest properties in all of Mayfair, so that possibility seems remote. There was an odd sound whilst we were there, though. A howling if I had to name it. Mrs St Harlow said that they had just taken over the care of a small puppy and were trying to train the animal. Her sisters looked less than comfortable with the explanation, however, and

I got the feeling they were relieved to see us go. Not Leonora, of course. Rodney and she existed in a space all of their own and I have never seen my brother so happy.'

'Is it wise to encourage him, do you think?' Nat asked the question.

'You refer to Mrs St Harlow's past, no doubt, and the unfortunate accident at Medlands.'

'It was widely known that they were not happy. Charles had apparently said something of his wife expressing her desire for his early demise not long before he died. His friends testified that she harassed and badgered him all of the time, a woman who was never content with all the gifts that he was showering upon her. By all accounts from the London jewellers and suchlike, there were many.'

'Which friends?' Stephen joined in the conversation.

'Freddy Delsarte and his cronies were amongst their number, if I recall.'

'Delsarte waylaid Mrs St Harlow at the ball. She had bruises on her wrist from his grip.'

'Perhaps he is another of her disenchanted lovers, then. The parties they held at Medlands were notorious.' Nat used a tone that was unusual. Stephen had heard the same cadence when information was being extracted from a difficult informant, the undercurrents of deception held within.

'I thought it brave of her to even attend, Hawk.' Cassie's voice resonated with a definite query.

'She has three sisters to marry off. That would make a warrior out of any woman.' Hawkhurst remembered her antics above Taylor's Gap.

'Yet she makes no effort at all to give her side of the story. If she was pardoned by the courts, she must be innocent.'

'Or she had a good lawyer,' Nathaniel interjected and Stephen could hear his impatience with the whole thing. 'Charles was a man who none of us liked and Mrs St Harlow is a woman whom society detests. Perhaps they suited each other entirely.'

'I don't think I detest her,' Cassie interrupted. 'I think, under other circumstances, we might have been friends. You had a waltz together, Hawk. What do you make of her character?'

She kisses well and goes to pieces on the smallest of caresses.

He wondered what would be said should he voice such things and remained quiet.

'I barely know her.' Stephen did not wish to be drawn into Cassandra's wiles by admitting more and when the conversation meandered on to other topics, he was pleased.

On Monday afternoon, despite willing himself not to, Hawk found himself in the park watching for the conveyance containing Aurelia St Harlow and her father. Why he did not just dismiss the woman from his notice was beyond his understanding but there it was, logic lost beneath a will that had forgotten what was good for him.

He did not have long to wait before they came, Aurelia in her black bombazine with a matching hat and her father tucked in beside her in the open landau. She chatted and laughed, the driver on the front box dressed in the livery of the stables complex in Davies Mews and the horses a well-matched pair of greys.

The senior Beauchamp must be a gifted conversationalist, Stephen thought, as he caught her laughter on the wind, for he had never seen Aurelia St Harlow look so animated. He hated the way his body responded to the sound and bit down in irritation.

Below this thought, however, another one less generous tumbled, born from his years of observing people closely, he supposed, and from a lifetime of finding the wrong in things.

He could not see her father's lips moving in the spaces when his daughter did not speak and though he craned forward to watch more closely as they returned around the path for a second time, he was beginning to get the feeling that the gaiety of this carriage ride was a sham.

For whom? His eyes took in various lords and ladies gracing the park, the busiest time of the day, and although other conveyances slowed down to speak to those who might hail them, the Beauchamp carriage maintained a steady speed and a one-sided conversation for three whole passes around.

Then it simply left, gliding through the gates with all the grace of a completed outing, the horses perfectly in time and undoubtedly barely stretched.

Would Aurelia St Harlow never stop surprising him and why would she be bent on such a show?

Rodney Northrup chose that moment to saunter over towards him. The lad looked happier than he had looked for a long while and Hawk guessed his joyous admiration of Miss Leonora Beauchamp to have some hand in such newly found cheerfulness.

'Lord Hawkhurst. I have not seen you here before at this hour of the day. You have just missed Mrs St Harlow and her father. They left not more than a brace of minutes ago.'

Stephen decided to play along. 'I had heard they frequented the park on a Monday. I expect you were here to catch sight of the sister…Leonora, is it not?'

'Oh, Miss Leonora never accompanies them. It is always just Mrs St Harlow and her father.'

'I see,' Stephen returned. And he did.

With only the two of them in the carriage no one would stop to talk. Curious acquaintances would be a danger to any hidden secret and as Aurelia so religiously rebuffed anyone who might offer more than a glance, she and her father stayed safe from closer attention. Was Braeburn House entailed? No one had seen Richard Beauchamp in any company save that of his daughter in years. Could Aurelia St Harlow have kept any inti-

mation of her father being ill a secret to protect the inheritance of her three unmarried
sisters? Such a shield was exactly the sort
of thing he knew she might have held on to,
safeguarding any change detrimental to her
siblings' chance of a good marriage. Braeburn House was a prosperous address and
the affluent and moneyed of the *ton* would
easily be impressed.

He wished then that he might have stepped
forwards and seen what it was she would
have done. Part of him imagined the driver
to be instructed by her to merely run down
anyone who had the effrontery to approach
them. Hawkhurst swallowed back chagrin
and listened to Rodney.

'Cassie said that you should be receiving
an invitation to her party and that you were
to make sure you come. You have missed
many of her soirées, she said, and she wants
you to be at this one.'

Normally he had no interest in such gatherings and avoided them like the plague, but
she had mentioned the same celebration to
Mrs St Harlow at his ball and by her account
the invitation had been accepted.

He shrugged and looked away, watching
as other carriages pulled up and down the

concourse and wishing he might see the only
one that had caught his attention return.

Aurelia had seen Hawkhurst standing
against a gate on the path on the far side of
the park. She knew it was he by his stance
and the breadth of his shoulders and by an
awareness that disturbed every part of her
no matter what distance lay between them.

Nerves had made her more animated than
she usually was as his eyes had followed the
coach, once, twice, three times around the
track. He had spoken to no one as he had observed them, but his indolence belied a quieter interest. She made certain that she had
turned her head away from him each time
they had come closer, not wanting to see his
eyes shadowed with questions.

Rodney Northrup had approached him
right at the end of her time there, his happy
uncomplicated demeanour such a direct contrast to Stephen Hawkhurst's complexity.

Papa had spoken only occasionally, a
man who would loathe such a spectacle of
deception were he to know of it. She was
only pleased he did not close his eyes and
sleep as he did now for much of the time at
home—his way, she supposed, of dealing

with a world he no longer had any comprehension of. Or howl at something that frightened him.

The muscles in her cheeks ached from fix-
ing a smile with such an unrelenting pressure and she bit down upon worry. Every
week she hoped that they would not be waylaid by some well-meaning soul, some acquaintance with enough curiosity to uncover
all that she sought to hide.

The walk home from the stables in Davies
Mews was becoming a more harried pathway each time they traversed it. She could
not be sure that her father could manage any
of it for much longer, his gait more laboured
and slower every Monday afternoon.

Tears pricked the back of her eyes and she
willed them away, useless emotional bag-
gage that she had dispensed with years ago.
She was the only one who might see this
family through to a secure future and with
the growing profits she was garnering from
the silks it would only be a matter of months
before safety would be gained.

Hawkhurst carried a cane today and he
had leant upon it with more than a gentle
force. Had he been wounded recently or
was this an older injury? A great part of her

wished that she might have been able to stop and speak with him and pretend that just for a moment she was a high-born lady of consequence who would have made him a perfect wife.

Such an illusion was shattered completely when they gained the stables and the master of the books strode forwards to tell them that as the cost of an afternoon rental had just been increased he could no longer keep a carriage free if the payment was not given monthly.

So many pounds, Aurelia thought, adding the sum in her head. She still had the diamond pendant, though, and the pawnbrokers had offered her a sum that would see the charade through to at least October. By then she was certain the new lucrative contracts she had garnered would be trickling through.

'This way, Papa,' she encouraged her father as he turned in the wrong direction.

Uncoupling her pendant, she held it tightly in her hand, liking the feel of the warm and familiar shape of the piece against her skin. Her grandmother had given the necklace to her on her deathbed—it was a treasured family heirloom.

There was a pawnshop in the city that favoured the older style of jewellery. She would visit it tomorrow.

Chapter Six

Alexander Shavvon was unhappy as he paced up and down the small room.

'France needs to be contained and yet all information suggests otherwise, for already Louis Napoleon has expanded into Indo-China. If Lord Palmerston is not careful the *Entente Cordiale* fashioned under Guizot will return to bite the hand of the one that feeds it.'

Hawkhurst was not as certain as Shavvon of the direction of Francophile expansionism and fault. 'If I were determining policy, I would be keeping an eye on Prussia and the Germanic states, sir. All of my reading suggests the prospect of a United Germany, which would be a lot harder to contain than a beaten France.'

'Your uncle, of course, might not agree with you, Lord Hawkhurst. He knew first-hand the might of Napoleon and if we had not defeated the dictator at Waterloo, England would be a very different place now.'

'Perhaps it is becoming that different place already.'

'Talk to Alfred and see just what it is France is capable of and you might change your mind. You are too young to remember the fear engendered by our nearest neighbour in the Peninsular Campaigns, but it was a hit-and-miss affair as to which way it went and the British would never again wish for the like.'

Such stilted discourse made Stephen wary and he knew that his days in the clutches of the British Service were numbered. He had ceased to be a citizen of the brokered threat Lord Palmerston seemed to endlessly foster and all he wanted was the chance to head to one of his remote family estates and live life.

Well and quietly, walking into a future with nothing tied back into the past. Nothing sordid and chancy and dissolute!

He breathed out hard as the face of Aurelia

St Harlow came to mind. She wandered into his dreams at night, too, now, when his mind was least resistant and the call of her body against his at its most apparent, the generous heaviness of her bosom well remembered. Swearing under his breath, he concentrated again on what was being said by Shavvon.

'Frederick Delsarte and his mob have been seen hanging around a warehouse in Park Street in the Limestone Hole area and they have known associations in Paris. It seems they may be using the legalised trade of cloth to send and receive information.' He handed Stephen a sheet of paper with the details on it. 'Those who are helping him do so probably have some French connection and imagine themselves hard done by by the English Government. If we can catch them in the act, we can string them up, quietly, of course, and with as little public awareness as possible.'

Hawkhurst nodded. It was always the same, this game of espionage played out behind the scenes of a virtuous and wholesome society, the dark secrets of corruption snapped off before they had the chance to taint it.

His world.

Sometimes he wondered if he would ever truly be able to struggle back up into the one people like Elizabeth Berkeley inhabited, untouched by any iniquity.

'If you can manage to get into the channel of communication, let me know before you shut it down.'

'So you have time to turn the other cheek?'

Shavvon began to laugh. 'You are the best agent we have, Hawkhurst. I don't want you lost.'

Lost like his brother and all the others he had started with. For a while now Stephen had wished the end would come, quickly, in the shape of a bullet, neither painful nor lingering, just a true clear shot and then nothing. If Shavvon recognised such ennui, he did not say so as he turned to the pile of papers on his desk. Expedience had the look of a careless nonchalance and Hawkhurst was so very tired of it, this lie of his life, foundering in the shallows of evil.

'One day soon I will not be back.' The words were quietly said as he let himself out.

Henry Kerslake was late and worry gnawed as Aurelia waited for him. It was cold and what light there was would soon begin to fade. If he did not come within the half hour she would leave for home, for her father had been ill this morning and she was wanting to see that the fever he had woken with had not worsened.

Her teeth bit at her nails and she fisted her fingers when she realised what she was doing. Agitation had marked many areas of her body now, she thought—her hands, her stomach with a constant nervous ache and her face, the tension written deeply into lines of ugliness.

Beautiful. Hawkhurst had called her such, but he was a man who had wanted more when he said it and what male would not use falsity in such a situation?

She shook her head hard at this errant nonsense for where was such an idea leading? She had been mortified by both her reaction to his kiss at Taylor's Gap and her heightened sense of Hawkhurst as he had sat with her in the carriage. Charles's betrayals were stretched thin across the veneer she had so successfully erected and she knew that any break would destroy everything in the same way that it had once before.

The sweet smell of opium smoke curling from a pipe and Charles's eyes upon her, glittering bright and furtive. She had allowed him the right to pull the gown away from her breasts so that flesh spilled out into the air, cold in the autumn evening. She had trusted her husband, relied on his honour and his principles, the band of gold around his finger denoting all that she had promised him.

Foolish false troths. It had taken her only one night to understand his depravity.

The noise of feet made her turn and, as the door opened, she saw that Henry Kerslake had finally arrived. He looked distracted and tired, the large bag he carried over his shoulder rubbing a dent into his over-cloak.

'The jacquards took longer than I had imagined they would to sample. Although the punched cards make the patterns more intricate, they are slow to set up.' Opening the buckles on the bag, he brought out a swathe of cloth, flowers and leaves that owed much to the influence of Japan spilling forth.

'Godwin had his hand in the design, Mrs St Harlow, but I have strengthened the colours myself. What do you think?'

'The stylised motifs are…unusual, though the Oriental taste is gaining in attraction.' To her eye the shades were too lurid and the shapes too foreign, but her own Louis schemes garlanded in blossom were falling in demand and she knew that they had to widen their range.

'No one else in Macclesfield is doing anything like it yet, so if we hit the market quickly we will be ahead of them all.'

His sentiment heartened her. With the mooted reopening of the trade routes to Japan, interest in the East had escalated and the furniture being turned out by eminent manufacturers reflected the change. She had begun to see bamboo used in the new mass-produced chairs and tables, something silk patterns such as these ones would complement exactly and she was enough of a businesswoman to understand the necessity of diversity.

Renaissance splendour, Gothic arches, gilded rococo boiseries, French roses and now a simpler lightness from a country far from Europe. Her own designs stood alongside those from the more famous houses, but with the limited time she had to produce them she was beginning to depend on Henry and his 'fashionable finds' more and more. The thought concerned her, for if she lost control, everything would be forfeited.

There was nothing to be done, however, and as a woman she was bound to use a man as a front-person no matter how liberal-minded those she was doing business with purported to be. Victorian sensibilities could not be changed in a moment, even though the rumblings of emancipation were beginning to be heard more plainly.

Not for her, though, the luxury of free hours to pursue a lofty cause all in the name of womanhood. Time was her enemy and had been for a long while, though she was becoming most adept at using it more effectively.

'Put the Little Street Mill into the production of the Japanese-patterned silks and keep the Chester Street Mill producing the French-styled roses.'

Henry Kerslake did not look pleased. 'You might regret not moving more quickly upon this matter, Mrs St Harlow.'

Irritation bloomed at his criticism, but the relationship between her and Henry Kerslake had been foundering just as certainly as their profits had been increasing. Another few months and she could sell the business at a good advantage. Aurelia was more and more desperate for that time to come.

'I met a man on the way in who was asking questions about the sort of cargo we bring in here each month. I told him what I knew and he went on his way.'

'Did he talk to others around here as well?'

'I don't know.'

Aurelia felt rattled by the news. A few of her designs had gone missing lately as had a book of invoices detailing payments pending, the new contracts secured detailed in pounds and pence. Could this person have had something to do with that? Perhaps another mill was on the prowl to see what it was they were to produce next. They had been lucky in their choices of design so far and mayhap this had been noticed by a less successful venture.

Some mills had failed even in the four years she had been in business, their warehouses empty and still, the slumps and booms that were so much a part of the English silk industry taking their toll. She wished there could have been someone to talk over these problems with, someone to give her guidance and advice, but her father's mind had long since dwelt in a place where no one could reach him and her three sisters' world encompassed none of this. Realising she was again biting her nails, Aurelia stopped. She would place sturdier locks on all of the doors and pray that such measures would be sufficient deterrent.

Henry Kerslake was not quite finished, however. 'The stranger had that unmistakable air of wealth about him, if you ask me, Mrs St Harlow.'

Shock reverberated through her. 'What did he look like?'

'Tall with dark hair and he moved in the way of a man who knows exactly where he is going.'

Lord Hawkhurst? Could it possibly be him? Had he been making enquiries about her that had led him back here? Danger made her breath shallow, although underneath some other small feeling blossomed quietly. She might see him again. He could be here right now, outside somewhere watching. Her glance went to the window, but there was only stillness, the grounds around the warehouse empty.

Fingering the silk on the table before her, she tried to settle back into some sort of work, but the colours and patterns swam into nothingness and all she could see were the golden eyes of a man who had begun to invade her night-time thoughts.

She was therefore pleased when Henry looked at his timepiece and packed up his things, in preparation for a meeting in town with one of the suppliers of buttons.

'I have left orders in the box for you to sort through, Mrs St Harlow. Dickens & Jones want extras of the fine, blue, hand-made shawls for their shop in Regent Street. Perhaps we might need to employ more staff at Chester Street to cope?'

Aurelia winced. Another problem that she would have to deal with quickly. Was there no end to her worries today? She was pleased when Kerslake left and a rare silence enfolded her.

She did not feel like working, fidgety nervousness making her stand, a prickling feeling raising the fine hair on her forearms. She was still at the window a few moments later when a knock on the door took her attention. Thinking it to be Kerslake, she opened it, but it was not him, and the air that she had just breathed in congealed at the back of her throat.

Chapter Seven

Mrs Aurelia St Harlow stood before him, a swathe of scarlet silk in her hands and wearing the same black dress Stephen had seen her in every time he'd met her.

'You?' Her voice could not have been more shocked, her mismatched eyes widened and fearful. 'What are you doing here?'

Hawkhurst had to smile at that because the question was exactly the one he was about to ask her and because there was no earthly reason why a well-to-do lady should be lurking in the run-down buildings on the back streets of the Limestone Hole warehouses.

Save one.

'You work here?' Everything had just got

a whole lot harder and the mission he had been sent on by the Service was in danger of being compromised entirely. His glance took in the bolts of fabric and the squares of colours and designs that littered a large wooden table in the middle of the room. Ledgers were piled up five high in a bookcase beside it and further off in one corner a dog stood chained to the wall, his teeth bared in grisly defiance.

'Down, Caesar!' The animal crouched uncertainly at her command, flecks of spittle around its jawline. Stephen got the feeling that if it could forsake its chains it would be at his throat in an instant; much like its mistress if the look on Aurelia St Harlow's face was anything to go by.

'A nice pet,' he drawled and stayed where he was.

'Protection,' she returned, the anger in her eyes boding badly. She neither asked him inside nor shut the door to keep him out.

An impasse. The sky solved the situation by suddenly opening, rain scudding in the wind towards them across the line of brick buildings drenching everything, and she allowed him through. The dog rose again on its haunches at his movement forwards, a low growl filling the room.

'He is not used to visitors.'

'I will stand by the door, then.'

'It might be wise.' When she smiled briefly the lines of worry melted into radiance and he drew in breath. God, Aurelia St Harlow's beauty held a sensuality that always surprised him and, doffing his hat, he placed it in front of his tight trousers, the effect she had on his anatomy singular and strong. Irritation mounted.

'I cannot remember my cousin delving into silks.'

'That is because he didn't.'

'You are saying this is your doing?'

'My father's family have manufactured silk buttons for a hundred years. It is in the Beauchamp blood.'

'And he approves?'

The quick tilt of her head worried him. She looked momentarily disappointed.

'Women these days are less likely to seek authorisation from the men around them, Lord Hawkhurst, for there is a new movement afoot that allows for women's emancipation. My late husband would have been more than horrified at any such thought, but there it is; I can work in any field of industry that I am competent in and no one can stop me.'

'Indeed?' The idea was beginning to occur to him that she was the most fearless female he had ever met. He could not even begin to imagine ladies such as Elizabeth Berkeley and her ilk secreting themselves in such a dangerous part of London with an animal who probably had feral wolf in its bloodlines.

A grimmer thought also surfaced.

Could she be the one sending information to France through the textile channels from England? His agent had been most specific that this office was the one from which the package of coded information had first come. He changed his tack entirely.

'Cassandra Lindsay was impressed by Leonora. She imagines her youngest brother to be in love.'

'Are you warning me, my lord?'

Hawkhurst felt a glimmer of respect for a woman who picked up so very quickly on the things said beneath other words. 'The marriage of your sister into a family of great note is something you have your heart set on. Nathaniel, however, would not thank me if there were secrets in the Beauchamp household that would cause even the slightest consternation to his wife. Or to his name.'

'There are not.'

Her scent filled the room, the particular aroma of violets and freshness.

'Yet I am trying to understand why a lady of means might wish to spend her days in a dusty warehouse sorting silks.'

Colouring, she looked away, guilt marking the movement.

His cousin's widow had French blood, giving her the will to help a country that was her mother's. She had told him her mother's nationality when he had first met her. The money in the business of secrets could also be substantial. Charles's estate had been sizeable as had her father's family's, but perhaps there was more at stake than riches. English society had in effect thrown her out on her head at the unexplained death of her husband and revenge was sweet in anyone's language.

Ice formed in his veins.

'It is most unusual for a woman of society to be involved in such endeavours.'

'Oh, one gets tired of tapestry and cross-stitch, my lord, and as I always liked design

I thought to try my hand at something more challenging.'

'You did not think to do this in a more conducive setting.' He looked pointedly at the dog.

'I am quite safe, Lord Hawkhurst, despite all you might think.'

'Do you work here alone?'

'No. There are two of us. My partner in the business, Mr Kerslake, has just left.' A blush darkened her cheeks.

'Kerslake is the man I spoke to earlier, I presume?' She nodded at his question and remained silent as he remembered the fellow. Ambitious. Good looking.

Damn. Perhaps there was more than a working relationship between them, ensconced as they were in a room far from the watchful eyes of others.

Her hair was uncovered today and the red in it was astonishing. He wanted to cross the space between them and hold the colour to the light, a flame of scarlet much the same shade as the silk trailing from her fingers. Here in the docklands, she was as far from the woman he had kissed as she could be, independence and the uncompromising strategies of business guarding any softer words.

She wanted him gone, too. He could see this from the way she tapped her foot against the floor, like a musician might measure the time in a song until it was finished.

'I would prefer it, my lord, if you could keep the knowledge of my small concern here to yourself.' She breathed out a deep sigh to punctuate her dilemma, her brow heavily creased and her shoulder drooping.

'And why should I do that, Mrs St Harlow?'

'Society finds unconventional women… perturbing. And it has been my experience that what they don't understand they generally also do not like.' The tone of her voice mimicked that of Elizabeth's friends, breathless and wavering. He laughed, the sound filling the room around them and the vulnerable and dejected air of a second ago disappeared into plain anger as her eyes flinted.

Hawkhurst swore under his breath. A self-effacing timid demeanour did not suit Aurelia St Harlow at all, this Boadicea of the Victorian drawing rooms who fought for an advantageous alliance for her younger sister despite a reputation that would have kept others as far from any public communion as they could go.

'I like you better when you do not simper, Mrs St Harlow.'

A half smile crept up on to full rounded lips. One small curl had escaped the confines of her tightly bound hair and fell across her throat on to the generous curve of her bosom. He drew his eyes back to her face, feeling like he had as a green boy, caught in the act of ogling. But she was not yet finished with plying her sister's case. This time there was no tone of supplication evident at all.

'Lady Lindsay is more than willing to consider the match and any intervention from you could only harm a relationship which both my sister and Mr Northrup wish to pursue.'

'The dubious woes of star-crossed lovers are hardly my concern!' He hated the cynicism he could hear so plainly, but he was a man who did not like the unexplained, and so far everything about Mrs St Harlow confused him.

She worked in a warehouse and lived in one of the most expensive town houses in Mayfair, a residence well furnished and appointed according to Cassie Lindsay; yet her hands were marked with the vestiges of a labour that had nothing at all to do with her confessed design work on light silk.

'I saw you the other day in the park with your father. The greys were very fine.'

'The enjoyment of good horseflesh is one of Papa's passions.'

She took a breath and held it, her fingers laced together in a tight white line. At breaking point, he deduced, the pulse of a vein in her throat denoting tension.

'Indeed, he looked most amused by the conversation. Almost too amused, were I to place a point upon it.'

'I do not know what you mean, my lord.'

'Are the Beauchamp properties entailed?'

The very blood simply went from her face, one moment flushed and the next pale.

'Did Cousin James send you here?'

He laughed at that. 'Nothing so prosaic, I am afraid, though I am guessing that this man is the one your father's title and lands will pass to when he dies or if he is no longer capable of performing his expected duties.'

To that she made no response.

'Charles was a wealthy man and a generous one by all accounts. Surely, as his wife, you did very well on his death?'

Again she remained quiet.

'I can hear it from you, Aurelia, or I can instruct my lawyers to look into my cousin's accounts. I would prefer it if you told me.'

After a few seconds she began to speak, softly at first, but then gaining in volume. 'My husband's estate was mortgaged up to the hilt. I have been trying to pay back the creditors I personally took food and services from ever since he died.'

Suddenly he understood. 'With the money gained from silk?' Lord, why had he not guessed? She had worn the same serviceable dress nearly every time he had met her and the gifts of jewellery from Charles which Nat had spoken of were never anywhere in sight. Today, even the pendant he had seen about her neck every other time he had met her was gone. Unwillingly, he supposed. Her fingers had crept to her throat on several occasions during the conversation, dropping to her sides when they discovered the loss. Had she pawned the piece for quick cash?

'There are two mills in Macclesfield and the warehouse here in Park Street. The trade is beginning to be profitable and will continue to stay so if I can only...' She petered out, the words simply stopping on her tongue.

'Keep your father's state of health a secret?'

The shock in her eyes was underlined by fear as she stepped back. He had the feeling that she might have been planning to simply walk out of the door, but had then thought better of it, choosing instead to defend herself with words.

'A lord contemplating jumping from a cliff to solve the problems of the world that ailed him might be perceived by any business partners as a risk.'

'Touché!'

He tried to keep his tone light, an airy unconcern visible, but underneath another truth rose into life. She would sacrifice herself for her father and for her family and if anyone got in her way…?

'You would spread such a lie?'

'It depends on whether you interpret my father's sickness as influenza or dementia.'

An ultimatum of protection. There was some damned fine sense of poignancy in such a stance and in his line of business it had been a while since he had met another who might do the same.

She knew she had made a mistake as soon as he drew back, but there was nothing she could do about any of it. He would hate her now, that much at least was obvious, the lighter play between them dissolved in the message of her threat.

Ruin me and I will ruin you!

She loathed herself for even thinking to use such a warning and yet the faces of those she supported came to mind: Papa, Leonora, Harriet and Prudence, and John with his wife Mary.

And in Paris… Aurelia shook her head. No, she would not dwell on this now, a man who seemed to read her very mind standing before her.

Twenty-six and forever adrift from society.

'If it is money you need…'

She broke into his words even before he had finished them, unwilling to hear the offer. 'I need only your confidence, Lord Hawkhurst.' The dog growled at her tone.

'Then you have it.' His words were clipped short and he was gone even before she had time to answer. As the door shut behind him, Aurelia closed her eyes. He had looked at her as if she were…unknown, the undercurrents between them disappearing into simple loathing. The ache of it stabbed quick for in the nights after everyone had found their beds and the moon was high she had dreamed there might be something finer, something real and right and true. As she shook her head hard, the betrayal of hope was a timely reminder of why she had not sought out the company of others in the years since Charles's accident.

The shaped sharp end of the oak branch had pointed upwards, all the intentions of death in its careful placement. The brush before the jump had been so precisely angled, hiding everything, and she had been most vigilant in shielding John from the heavy hand of the law when it was determined he was the last person to be seen in the vicinity. The questions had come, of course, but the true answers had been lost in the interim, clues to the truth gone for ever and only conjecture left.

Sitting at the table, she unlocked a drawer at the very bottom of her desk and drew out a pouch of leather wrapped in silk. She knew that Lord Hawkhurst had not been here for a casual or idle chat; she had seen it in his stance and heard it in all the things he had not said.

'Ahh, mon Dieu, qu'est-ce que je fais maintenant?'

Oh, my God, what should I do now?

Drawing out the newest missive from Paris, Aurelia understood the need to be even more careful than she usually was when she passed the letter on.

She remembered Sylvienne's wide and frightened eyes when they had last met in Paris, the furtive looks across her shoulder as her mother had explained she did not feel safe.

Freddy Delsarte had been there, of course, his own brand of cunning gleaming in his eyes, the secrets of the daughter of a well-respected and wealthy English gentleman pointing to a lucrative blackmail.

Another responsibility. A further problem. Aurelia felt as though she was a tightrope walker poised on a thin rope above chaos and despair.

Chapter Eight

Aurelia met Stephen Hawkhurst in the library in Bond Street on Tuesday morning, almost falling over him as she rounded one aisle. His height and strength in the smallness of Hookham's seemed out of place here, a warrior amidst the formality of Society's quieter pursuits.

She wished she had worn her light blue dress, as even to her own uncritical eye the black bombazine did her skin little favour. Pushing such ridiculous vanity aside, she waited, for after their conversation at Park Street there could be little he wanted to say to her ever again.

'I hope your father's influenza is abating, Mrs St Harlow.'

So that was how he would play it. She felt her cheeks flush red. 'Indeed it is, my lord.' Her hands clutched a book of flowers drawn as lithographs on to thin tissue and further afield she noticed a couple of women looking their way.

Nay, his way, she amended, their expressions having the same sort of interest she had perceived on most of the female guests at his ball.

When he beckoned her to follow him towards the end of the room she went uncertainly, pleased that the onlookers were blocked from her view by a tall shelf.

'I have been giving the…situation with your father some thought.'

Shaking her head, she turned to leave, but he caught her arm and held it, the grip of his fingers allowing her to go nowhere.

'Could you speak with your cousin and gain his approval in ensuring your family's living situation is more stable? Surely if such a thing were to leave you destitute the man might consider such an action.'

'Or he might throw us out tomorrow.'

'He seems reasonable enough.'

'You have checked up on him?' Horror

and anger made her voice rise a good few octaves.

'Mr James Beauchamp has a name for being a fair and equitable man.'

'No.'

'He is also a friend of Rodney Northrup's.'

'One can be a respected man or a beloved friend and still have a penchant for that which has never been enjoyed.'

'From where I stand there seems more than enough to share and I am certain your family would be relieved to see you at home a little more often.'

'No.' The single word was louder this time as she broke off contact between them, danger sprouting from such intransigence. Did Lord Stephen Hawkhurst really expect just to waltz into her life and change it as if it were a knitting pattern, easy and simple? She knew what would happen next. Of course she did. If Mr James Beauchamp came to the house in the guise of a distant cousin inclined to help, everything would change.

They would all have to be grateful to him and the whims of an unmarried twenty-seven-year-old man might include the wish for a wife. Then Leonora or Prudence or Harriet would be sacrificed for the greater good of the family, and each of them would go without a whimper to protect her. She knew this as truly as she knew the night followed the day because all year the whispers she heard when the others thought she was not listening had been about their worries for her.

Aurelia works too hard. If only we could find a way to help her.

Well, the silks were beginning to pay and the new completed designs were beautiful and different. Another few months and everything would be possible. The only tripping block stood before her in Hookham's lending library in the large form of the implacable Lord Stephen Hawkhurst and he did not look pleased.

'How many other sisters do you have?'

'Two. Prudence and Harriet are twins.'

'Do they look like you?'

'No. They are much prettier, for they favour Leonora and—'

A ripe swear word broke off her sentence.

'Charles was a man who appreciated beauty in women. Surely he let you know of the qualities in yourself that he admired?'

'Oh, indeed he did.' She took away the sting in the words by sheer dint of will. He admired women who would do things in the bedroom that even prostitutes in the East End of London might have blushed at and he had simply abandoned her on his estate in the far north when she had refused to take part in any of it. Even the servants he had left her with had been instructed to be of as little help as possible until she came around to understanding what the words 'I promise to obey' meant in their hastily completed marriage.

The first few nights alone had been the worst. After that she had thanked the Lord for the distance between her new abode and her new husband and for the independence that naturally followed. Aye, her freedoms had been hard won and she was not about to give them up now to anyone.

'Such problems are mine to solve, my lord.' Aurelia could barely get the words out, so desperate was she to escape, and the headache she had had all morning began to play upon her vision. 'The silk trade is shaping up well and in a few months I am certain I shall be—'

'Dead and buried by the looks of the dark rings beneath your eyes.'

Glancing down, she resisted the urge to

lift her fingers to her face. She had hardly
slept for days, the difficulty of everything
increased somehow by all the consequences
of the Hawkhurst ball. Leonora and Rodney. Cassandra Lindsay and her invitation
to a country-house party. The carriage ride
home where she had understood for the first
time in her life what it was to be attracted
to a man.

Not just any man, either, but this one before her, his eyes filled with certainty.

'What if Lady Lindsay brought your sisters out and I footed the bill?'

Aurelia could not believe what she had
just heard and shock made her step back.

'I could never accept such an offer.'

'Why not? You were married to my cousin
and as the head of the Hawkhurst family I
would be most remiss to leave you floundering financially as a widow.'

'I am hardly a relative you might be expected to nurture, my lord, and people would
talk.'

'They talk now, Aurelia.'

His eyes were softened in the grey light of
a gloomy London afternoon and she thought
he had never looked more beautiful.

'I should tell you that Cassandra Lindsay broached the subject with me yesterday. She has met your sisters, apparently, and was most impressed by them.'

'Oh.' The wind was taken from her sails as she tried to decide exactly what to do.

Turning away, she looked out of the window, a squally rain shower pushing a stray sheet of paper down the street. Once, she would have accepted such help with barely a backward thought. Once, hopes and dreams had been written in her eyes just as they were now in Leonora's, and the future had looked bright. She had worn colourful gowns, then, gowns to highlight the shade of her hair and the dashing Mr Charles St Harlow, newly returned from the Americas, had been entranced.

For all of a month. The anger in her grew with the shame.

'Would Lady Elizabeth Berkeley not find such patronage odd, given you are already promised to her in marriage?'

'Who told you that?'

'Lady Lindsay herself. At your ball.'

A single muscle rippled in his jaw, but he did not speak.

'I do not wish to make matters difficult for you, but if I agree to such a thing it would only be on the grounds that I would pay you back.'

'Very well.'

'When I sell my silk business. I would write out a vowel, of course, though I understand if you would prefer to involve a lawyer…'

'I wouldn't.'

Flustered at the clipped tone in his words, she held out her hand. 'Do we shake on it, then?'

His fingers came across her own, warm and strong, the connection even here in a public library and under the strictest terms of trade still having the capacity to make her…breathless.

'I shall keep a careful tally of all expenses, Lord Hawkhurst.'

His pupils darkened with shards of gold splintering on the edge. Predatory and watchful, yet Aurelia could not care.

He did not break his grip and she did not loosen hers, either. Rather, here in the quiet corner of a room of knowledge she wished she was standing instead on the top of Taylor's Gap with no one around for miles and all the reason in the world to thank him properly.

He had shown her what a kiss could feel like, once, and she wanted that again. Her face flushed with the effort of holding back and for the first time she saw a hint of uncertainty cross his brow as he brought her hand upwards and placed his lips upon her skin in the smallest of caresses. His tongue against the juncture of her fingers was soft and real, saying much in the hidden quiet of honesty.

'I don't know what burns between us, Mrs St Harlow, but there will come a time when we shall not have the will to stop it, I can promise you that.'

There, the words were said, falling against lies and covering them with a softer edge, like snow across the jagged sharp of rocks.

Only truth. The lump in her throat made her swallow as she tried to find an answer, but what indeed could she say? If she agreed, then only ruin would follow, and if she didn't…

She could not speak, even with everything held in a balance, and he let her hand go and took a pace backwards.

The heavy fall of feet made them turn as a woman rounded the corner a good twenty feet away and proceeded towards them and Aurelia gained the distinct impression that he had heard her coming well before the lady came into sight.

'Lord Hawkhurst, what a delight to see you here.' Her smile was bright until her glance passed over Aurelia's face, and the sheen of it flattened.

'Lady Allum.' Hawkhurst's detachment was back, easily in place, and Aurelia had to marvel at the way he changed so quickly from one thing to another. She feared her own expression was nowhere near as schooled. 'Might I introduce Mrs St Harlow to you?'

Caught, the woman finally made eye contact, a furtive quick glance telling Aurelia that she believed all that had been said about her. Today the criticism hurt in a way it seldom had before.

'Lady Berkeley said that she was hoping to have you over for dinner on Saturday, Lord Hawkhurst. It is a small and select gathering, from all that I hear. Her daughter Elizabeth was particularly looking forward to the event.'

'I have already sent word that I cannot be present, my lady, as I shall be away from London all week.'

As the woman spoke again of another

assembly she wanted Hawkhurst to attend Aurelia used the conversation to simply excuse herself and walk away, the sound of her shoes on the polished parquet flooring marking her retreat. And then she was outside, the façade of the library tall against a dark and rain-washed sky. Hailing a passing hansom cab, she tried to decide exactly what she should do about the enigmatic and menacing Lord Stephen Hawkhurst, the beat of her heart quickening as she remembered his last words to her.

I don't know what burns between us, Mrs St Harlow...

So he felt it, too, this breathless intensity taking all that was ordinary and commonplace away and replacing it with...what? She stopped, searching for the right word, but it would not come in the way she wanted it and so her mind moved on.

He was due to marry one of the most beautiful debutantes of the Season and she was an outcast, for ever shut away from proper society. Nay, there could be nothing at all between them and to dream otherwise would only lead to the disappointment she had already experienced too much of.

* * *

Stephen stalked into White's club in St James's Street, barely noticing the surroundings of plush leather chairs and numerous chandeliers. All he wanted was a drink to wipe out the desire that coursed through him and the irritation of Catherine Allum's untimely interruption.

Pure lust had made him admit that which should have been unspoken, but he wished he had kept his mouth shut even whilst imagining Aurelia's flame-red hair lying across his loins, the heavy abundance of her breasts in his palms and his mouth.

Swearing roundly, he took a seat by the fire, draping his legs with his frock coat so that others might not see the swelling he could feel pushing against superfine.

'A difficult day?'

He had not thought the seat opposite to be occupied, as it was turned at an angle away from the fire, but with a scrape of wood on parquet flooring Lucas Clairmont swivelled his chair, brandy being warmed by carefully cupped hands.

'You have the look of a man who has sparred with the opposite sex, Hawk, and lost. My bets are the lady in question is the enigmatic Mrs St Harlow for I doubt the timid Lady Elizabeth Berkeley could raise such a high temper in anyone.'

Despite his dilemma Stephen smiled and accepted a glass of the same drop from a passing waiter, draining the contents before trusting himself enough to speak. 'I met Mrs St Harlow unexpectedly at Hookham's library and I offered to bring her youngest sisters out with the help of Cassandra Lindsay. They are twins.'

'A very generous offer.'

'And one she wanted to refuse.'

Laughter made Stephen wish that he had said nothing at all. 'Only a good woman can get under your skin in that way, Hawk. My wife, Lillian, has the same capacity to make me wild with both fury and desire and all at the same time.'

'I never said that was how I felt.'

'Not in words, maybe, but there is something about your demeanour since the ball that is different....'

'It is provocation and exasperation, Lucas, and it all comes down to the impossible Mrs St Harlow.'

Luc finished his drink in one unbroken swallow. 'Nay, it is the unexpected compre-

hension of feelings only few inspire, Hawk.
If you listened to what's left of your heart,
you might just hear the music, and if you do
it will probably save you.'

'Lillian has turned you into a romantic,
Luc, and your advice is completely without
sense.'

But the strong liquor soured at the back
of Stephen's throat. For the first time in his
life he did not know exactly what to do with
a woman and it worried him. All of Luc's
talk of salvation rankled, too. Only innocence and purity might beat back the demons
that consumed him and Aurelia St Harlow
was no fresh-faced ingénue. His ruminations
were interrupted, however, by Luc's further
rhetoric.

'I ran into Lady Berkeley an hour or so
back. Her daughter is most distressed that
she may have offended you in some way at
your ball. She has not heard from you since,
it seems?'

'I have been busy.'

Leaning forwards Lucas lowered his
voice. 'There is something else that I think
you ought to know about your cousin's mysterious widow, Hawk. She visits St Bar-

tholomew's Hospital once a month to speak with a doctor named Giles Touillon.'

'French?'

'Indeed.'

The world spun inwards. Lord, Shavvon had sent him to the warehouses in the Limestone Hole to find a French connection and a disenfranchised traitor. Could Aurelia St Harlow be the leak? After a lifetime of spying Stephen had ceased to believe in the benevolent nature of mere coincidence. It was always so much more than that.

'You look…odd, Hawk. Are you well?'

'Very.' Stretching back in the chair, he smiled. Even before Lucas he erected barriers. The thought made him sadder than it ought to. 'If you see Lady Berkeley in the next day or two, Luc, could you tell her I shall call upon them at the end of the week for I have been summoned away north.'

'Problems at Atherton?'

'Life is always demanding its pound of flesh,' he returned, feeling in the answer that he had not quite lied.

A few hours later Hawk walked through the maze of alleyways between Katherine Street and Drury Lane, the stench of this poorer part of London rising in his nostrils. A woman's fan brushed his face and he warned her away, the age-old code of the streetwalker's offer lost in a smile where both gums and teeth had been eaten up by the mercury cure.

He was glad he had come in the guise of a sailor, the homespun of his clothes attracting little attention as he pulled the hat he wore further down upon his forehead.

Knocking on the door of a house on the corner of one of the small intertwining streets, he waited. Within a few seconds the bolts were slipped and he was allowed through, heavy locks refastened behind him.

'Phillips said ye'd come.' The man before him was small and wiry, a shock of red hair topping a freckled face.

'He's left the papers, then.' Stephen's words were tinged with the accent of the same slums.

'I need the words first. The ones you'd know to say.'

'Angliae notitia.'

A lamp flared and the corners of the modest room were bathed in light. A woman sat to one side on a small stool with a baby asleep on her lap.

'Not a peep, mind, to anyone. If you talk, me wife and I, we're as good as gone.'

'I understand.' Hawk brought the coins from his pocket, the profile of the Queen etched in bronze. 'There's more where this came from if you have anything else.' A flash of greed told him that the red-haired man probably did. Settling back, he crossed his legs in front of him. Experience had taught him patience in any negotiation and the art of biding his time. Information gathering had its own set of intricate rules, after all, and the first of them was to feign indifference.

'The one they call Delsarte and his cronies have been hanging around the warehouse. I ain't seen the woman do nothing with them, though. She just goes late back to that fancy home of hers up in Mayfair when she has finished and returns in the morning. As early as sin, I should say.'

'Have you ever seen her talking with them?'

'No.'

Stephen's glance went to the girl sitting to one side, but her eyes were cast downwards.

'There is something that I heard Delsarte say…' Stopping, he waited for a timely reminder and Hawk handed him another handful of coins. 'He said that he was going to Paris and that there was more money in it than this business could provide him with. Then the rain came down heavy so's that I couldn't listen no more. The woman he was talking to was from Mother Spence's place down Katherine Lane. A big dark-haired girl with patches, rouge and a long scar down her forearm. She might know more if ye asked her, though ye'd have to be careful as she was hanging on to him like he was a gift or something.'

'Did you get into the warehouse to look over the files?'

'No, not a chance to. The dog stops you when there's no one in. A big monster of a hound that lets everyone know he's there. I heard them mention a boat, though, last week, when I was following them home from the Black Boar. The *Meridian*. I checked and she's in at St Katherine's Dock.'

'You've done well.' Standing, Stephen placed a silver shilling on the table before him. 'For the babe,' he said as he collected his hat and left.

Nathaniel Lindsay was waiting for him in his library when he returned after eleven o'clock, and he had already finished a large amount of his best bottle of whisky.

'You are still at the game, then?' His eyes passed over the homespun as Stephen took off the woollen overcoat and hat.

'If you come uninvited, you have to take what is here without comment, Nat.' Finding a glass, Hawk poured himself a generous drink, pausing to enjoy the smooth taste of the golden liquid.

'Cassie sent me.'

'Why?'

'She thinks you need a talking to over your choice of women.'

'I thought your wife approved of Elizabeth Berkeley?'

Laughter echoed around the room. 'You would devour everything about that poor chit within a year, Stephen, and curse yourself for doing so.'

'Indeed?'

'Women are like this whisky, my friend. Find a full-bodied and complicated brew and it will suit you for ever. It worked for both Luc and me.'

The words fell into the silent warmth of the library, soft harbingers of persuasion.

'You are saying that the basis for a good marriage is a complicated woman?'

Nathaniel's hands flailed in the air. 'I am saying that I am worried about you, Stephen. All this…disguise and deception. It is making you sadder than you need to be.' He paused for a second before carrying on. 'Remember when your parents died and we were at school? How old were we then? You and Luc and I?'

'Thirteen.'

'Thirteen. And we said that we would always be family from then on. We made a promise cut into the skin at our wrists.' Pulling up the sleeve on his arm, he traced one finger over a thin white line. 'I pressed too hard and ended up in the clinic and you slept on the floor beside me for a week. I think if you had not been there holding my hand in the cold of the night I wouldn't have survived. Now it is my turn to make certain that you survive.'

With a frown Stephen looked down at his own hands, the nails filled with dirt from where he had scraped them along the earth on the driveway before his foray into the dark alleys off St Katherine's Row. Placing his drink down, he stood, walking to the window to look out into the darkness.

'I have already told Shavvon I am leaving.'

'When?'

'After this…case.'

'Your brother would be pleased were he still here.'

'Considering he died for the same cause that I am quitting, I highly doubt it.' The ferocity of the words surprised Hawk.

'Which is the sole reason that you have stayed in for so long. Daniel was killed because he didn't listen to reason just as you are not doing now.'

'No. He died because I didn't protect him.'

'You took a bullet in the thigh and spent a good portion of that summer in a coma and have limped ever since, for God's sake. Your brother died because neither he nor you could outrun bullets fired by a crazy Frenchman with little in the way of integrity. You did your best to save him, Hawk, and you have paid the price in pain ever since. It's time to let it go, let it all go and find the life Daniel was never able to live. It would not be a betrayal.'

Betrayal?

Life in the British Service had in effect once saved him, giving purpose and family to two young boys left without either. With their parents gone, Daniel and he had been rudderless until the steady sure hand of responsibility and duty had guided them on to a path which was significant and worthy. Such initial fealty now caused Hawk's conscience to burn, yet beneath, another need blazed brighter.

Aye, betrayal came in many forms.

That thought made Stephen look up. If he didn't change, he would die. Soon. Like his brother, disappearing into the hazy and shadowed world of espionage.

Today in the company of Aurelia St Harlow he had been honest, a chance taken without thought of recompense or reprisals. He had told her exactly what he thought lay between them and he had seen the answering flicker in her eyes—an unconstrained candour budding like green leaves from a bare and frozen branch in the first days of spring. New life. New hope in the peace of truth.

Outside, a shooting star fell from the heavens and for the first time since Stephen was a child he took a moment to wish upon it.

* * *

When he called upon Nat and Cassie two days later Aurelia St Harlow and her sister Leonora Beauchamp were ensconced in the small blue downstairs salon with Cassandra and her oldest sister, Maureen. Lady Delamont, the St Auburns' London neighbour, was also in attendance, a surprising fact given that Aurelia's reputation was hardly salubrious.

'Stephen.' Cassie crossed the room and drew him in before he could escape. 'Nathaniel said you might drop by and he instructed me to keep you here until he returned. Something about "a full and bodied brew", he said, though goodness only knows what that might mean. You know Lady Delamont, of course, and you remember Mrs St Harlow and her sister Leonora Beauchamp from your ball the other evening. Maureen is up for a week to stay with me, too.'

'Good afternoon, ladies.'

Leonora smiled at him and moved over, giving Stephen no choice but to find a seat in the middle of the sisters. Aurelia did not look at him.

'I'm glad you have returned early from

your journey north, Hawk,' Cassie said, with the vestige of a question.

Lady Delamont laughed and joined in the conversation. 'Lady Berkeley will be pleased, Hawk. The youngest Berkeley daughter is hoping to snare a husband before too long, I hear, and your name is amongst the mooted candidates for a dinner she has planned. A nice gal, Elizabeth, with good manners and a pleasing conversation. She will make someone a loyal and malleable wife.'

Somehow the words did not sound like praise and, chancing a quick look at Aurelia, Stephen saw how her hands had tightened on the velvet reticule in her lap.

'Oh, Hawk's name is on all the lists, Deborah.' Cassandra swatted away the gossip easily and began to speak instead of the gowns she had particularly noticed at his ball. In the ensuing chatter Stephen was able to turn and speak privately to Aurelia for the first time. Today her hair had been tightly plaited so that the redness looked darker. A small pin embellished with a ceramic flower sat above her ear.

'For a woman on society's blacklist, you

seem to be garnering a good number of invitations.'

Deliberation laced a small anger. 'As soon as my sisters are paired off I am certain I shan't get another one, my lord.'

'If you throw off the black shroud you might be surprised, Mrs St Harlow. The swatch of scarlet I saw you holding the other day, for example, would suit you admirably.'

The look on her face was dubious. 'Red against red, my lord?'

'Too tempting?' Stephen enjoyed the glint of confusion in her unusual eyes and, stretching out, he allowed his thigh to touch hers. She moved back as though she had been burned, leaving as much space between them as was possible, her left side plastered tightly against the armrest.

Her reaction was ridiculous. She knew that it was, but it was as though her body almost sizzled when he touched her. Please God that he might not have perceived her response, that he might not have noticed.

'Your father is looking well, Mrs St Harlow.' Lady Delamont leant across and spoke loudly. 'I always thought it a great pity when your mother left him. Sylvienne was very like you to look at, my dear, with her red hair and that quiet air of caution. I hear she lives in Paris now?'

'She does.'

'Surrounded by luxury and various beaus, no doubt? She had every eligible suitor in London after her in the Season, an original with a brain to match. Do give her my regards next time you see her.'

'I shall indeed, my lady.'

Aurelia's smile felt as artificial as her words. The last time she had visited Mama, Sylvienne had clung to her like a child needing comfort, the high price of her numerous lovers scrawled in heavy payment across her face. Abandoned by society. When she had asked after Papa the undercurrents of regret could be clearly heard in her question.

Perhaps she and her mother were more alike than she thought. Her mama had chosen to leave the right man and she had chosen to stay with the wrong one.

Unlucky in love.

The tiny phrase clung in her mind and Aurelia took in breath. She could not afford to let her guard down and Stephen Hawkhurst wasn't a man to be played with. He was dangerous and powerful and menacing. Even here, sitting still amongst a group of women she was aware of a thrumming authority, a man who had fought in wars and lived.

Aye, survival had a certain note of guilt that isolated one and made mockery of small concerns. It also brought a sadness that was palpable and haunting, the vestige of dark things that were never spoken of again.

Leonora's laughter dragged her from her thoughts.

'I should love to come, Lady Delamont, and I am certain my sister would, too.' Aurelia's heart sank. 'A masked ball, Lia. What could be more exciting?'

'The more, the merrier, Mrs St Harlow,' the old lady continued, 'and I have a roomful of masks collected over the years. If you should like to choose one with your sister I would be very pleased, for my late husband was a man who had a bent towards the absurd.'

'I have already chosen Nat's mask, Hawk.'

Aurelia heard the humour in Cassandra Lindsay's voice even as Hawk shifted in his seat. He did not look like a man who would enjoy a masked ball at all.

'Your husband used to favour these sorts of occasions, Mrs St Harlow.' Cassandra's sister spoke for the first time, her smile so sweet Aurelia knew she could not have meant insult.

'Indeed, it seems that Charles enjoyed anything that was underpinned with joviality.' At least Hawkhurst did not make the words sound like a compliment, which gave Aurelia a certain satisfaction.

Joviality. Her world spun for a moment as she was thrust back into her past, clinging to the hope that the man she had married might disappear into the air like a wisp of smoke.

Foolish, foolish choice.

The wedding band on her finger seemed to tighten of its own accord, like a noose, an uncompromising punishment that would always be with her.

She wished she was home, in her bedroom and away from the prying eyes of others, the talk of masked balls and happy times so very far away from all that she had known.

And endured.

'I hope none of your other sisters have caught your father's illness?' Cassandra Lindsay commented and Aurelia shook her head. To say more under the circumstances would be more than deceitful given Hawk's knowledge of the whole conundrum. Even

Leonora looked a little abashed and there was an awkward silence that was filled as Lady Delamont sought advice about a certain plant for her garden which she had been unable to find.

The conversation gave Aurelia a little time to regather her wits and squash down a rising panic. The tension emanating from Lord Hawkhurst next to her was almost palpable and she was pleased when Cassandra's husband appeared at the door.

Hawkhurst stood immediately, giving Aurelia the impression that his desire to be gone was almost as great as her own, and when he gave his farewells he did not look in her direction once.

With Stephen Hawkhurst departed, however, that particular sense of excitement disappeared with him and, looking at the clock in the corner of the room, Aurelia wondered just how many minutes would need to pass before she could leave, as well.

Chapter Nine

$\sim\!\!\infty\!\!\sim\!\!\infty\!\!\sim$

Aurelia took a letter to the hospital the next morning, the missive concealed in her reticule under other papers and a wide silk scarf. 'The last time,' she said to herself. This would be the last time she took such chances.

As she walked along the hospital corridor she was aware of a man observing her closely. When she smiled at him he fidgeted with something in his pocket and stood, disappearing around the corner at speed.

The sight of Freddy Delsarte as she came outside made her stiffen and she wondered what discovery might engender. Treason carried the death penalty and she knew that a defence of blackmail would not save her. She needed to get Sylvienne away from Paris and pay off Delsarte for his silence. Now Leonora's reputation was at stake, as well, and with the chance of happiness with Rodney Northrup almost coming to fruition… She stopped. Hawkhurst was circling in the Limestone Hole and in the places that society gathered; his connections with the secret service threaded into the verbal warnings he gave her, but for now it was Delsarte who wanted a word.

'You are the talk of the town, Mrs St Harlow, for Hawkhurst's ball has elevated you to the status of acceptable.'

'I have paid my dues, sir, as far as any legal requirements are concerned. Now I just wish to be left in peace.'

'Sylvienne might say the same.'

'Sylvienne?' Her voice was harsh even to her own ears. 'If you hurt even one hair on her head, Delsarte, I shall see to it that the truth about your questionable morality and allegiance is made known and you will be crucified for it.'

'A case of the pot calling the kettle black, Mrs St Harlow.'

She shook her head. 'Mama was a fool to have allowed you into her bed and I am even more of one to have been persuaded to deliver your letters. Lord Stephen Hawkhurst has been asking after your movements and it would be very easy to tell him all that I know.'

'Do that and you will be up there in the hanging noose alongside me, my dear. The British Government would have little sympathy for the daughter of a French whore.'

His anger made Aurelia take a step backwards. She was caught in the game as certainly as Delsarte was, her mother's welfare taking precedence over any allegiance to King or to country. Unsavoury, she knew, but Sylvienne was walking a knife edge and Aurelia could not let her fall.

The same man she had seen at the hospital suddenly crossed the street in front of them and Delsarte hurried away. Another player in the game of espionage and secrets? A further threat to the safety of her mother?

A note came in the late afternoon to Park Street as she was trying to fit in a few hours' work. The man who brought it had been instructed to wait for an answer and when she read the contents she was very glad Henry Kerslake was out and about.

Lord Hawkhurst wanted to see her and

had asked her to come in the provided carriage to his town house within the hour. Worrying about the implications of such a summons, Aurelia wiped the sweat from her palms on the skirt of her gown and looked up at the waiting servant.

Should she take a risk and go? She had heard rumours that Stephen Hawkhurst worked for the British Service though nothing had ever been confirmed. Perhaps he had come snooping because of the money she sent to France. Or perhaps he had something to tell her about the entailment of Braeburn House? The cold fear of discovery was choking and she knew it would be better to face him in private and alone than in some crowded soirée.

'I will need ten minutes before I could accompany you.' Aurelia was glad her voice sounded steady.

'Very well, ma'am.'

When he left she stood, the ridge of fur on Caesar's back raised in warning, his growls subsiding at his departure. 'I wish you could come…' she whispered and threw him a bone from a box beneath her desk. As the hound set down to the task of gnawing on it Aurelia crossed to the mirror in the small back room.

In the silvered reflection she looked both tired and shocked, her eyes uncannily like those of her mother's. Pinching her cheeks to try to produce some colour, she reached in habit for the pendant at her throat and stopped. No, it had gone, too, in the pretence and the deceit. There was nothing left to protect her family with but her wiles and her willpower.

Her coat hung on a hook by the door and as she pulled each button through she counted. Eight buttons. One for every year since she had met Charles St Harlow at the Redmonds' ball in Clarence Street. Eight years since she had been truly happy. Eight years since she had slept all through a night and woken in the morning with dreams that had made her smile.

The peal of the bells from the nearby church were loud as she came into the wind and with her head held high she allowed Hawkhurst's man to help her into the conveyance.

He should not see Aurelia St Harlow alone and so late in the day, but he wanted to look into her eyes as he asked her his questions, and know the truth. She had been seen today in the company of both the French doctor and Freddy Delsarte. He knew that if Shavvon were cognisant of such associations she would have already been brought in for questioning, such was the power of the Government's uneasiness over foreign collaborators.

His own desires and needs were another factor entirely, though he had never been a man to put himself first. But he was disconcerted by the blood in him that raced with possibility when everything about such a reaction was wrong.

He heard the carriage and stood, cursing a rising need.

'Mrs St Harlow, my lord,' Wilson introduced her and left, shutting the door behind himself firmly. Hawkhurst had already given orders that he was not to be disturbed under any circumstances and their relationship was such that he knew his instructions would be obeyed to the letter.

The heat from a well-stoked fire fell across the room and he watched as she unbuttoned her coat, her fingers shaking with the effort. After the heavy outer shell was discarded she carefully laid it upon the sofa beside her. In the silken lining he caught the same rows of stitched repair that seemed evident in all of her apparel.

'Thank you for coming.'

Her countenance was pale and drawn. When he indicated a chair to one side of the room she moved towards it, but did not sit. Her hands were gloveless and she wore no hat. 'Would you like a drink?'

'I seldom partake of any alcohol, my lord,' she returned, the formal edge on her words unnerving and her voice low.

'Wise,' he echoed as he emptied his own glass for the third time in as many minutes. 'You will excuse me for displaying no such abstinence.'

The slight nod of her head made him turn, her nose tip-tilted against the fire's flame and her dimples deep even when she did not smile. No wonder her cousin had offered her marriage in so short a time. Alfred had made it known that there had been many others vying for Aurelia Beauchamp's hand in her first Season and society had been as shocked as her father when she had chosen the self-indulgent Charles.

His cousin had whisked her from London the day of the wedding and she had not returned until her court appearance three years later, a devoted wife wrapped in widow's weeds and a hefty dose of sorrow.

For just a moment Stephen hardly knew where to begin. 'I could order tea if you would rather?' The quick shake of her head stopped him, so instead he tried another tack. 'How long have you worked in the Park Street warehouse?'

The spark in her eyes told him she had been expecting just such a question. 'Nearly four years. The mills at Macclesfield had lain vacant for a long time and I made use of them again. The warehouse here is the London base for the business.'

'And some of your silks come in from France?'

'Yes. With the lifting of import duties it is often cheaper to bring the hand-loomed silks in as an adjunct to what we can weave.'

'So you have contact with the traders in Paris?'

She hesitated before nodding. 'I do. Is there some problem with that, my lord?'

'No problem at all. Curiosity is just one of my many faults.'

'Somehow I doubt that. Palmerston has

the thought that all citizens with some link to France must be traitors.'

'You make it a point to understand politics?'

'I try to. The tariffs for the silk trade here are hefty, yet France enjoys little government intervention. Without a good knowledge of the changing pattern of the new bills and laws, my margins would suffer.'

Despite himself he laughed. 'My cousin could barely string a thought together about anything other than himself or fashion. How did he ever end up with a woman like you?'

A flash of panic crossed her face. 'I realise it is a difficult thing to understand, but I am trying to build a life again, my lord, trying to fashion a better existence for my family.'

'Why did you meet with Delsarte today, Aurelia?'

Anger whipped up fire in her eyes. 'You have had me followed?'

'England's safety comes with good intelligence.'

'Your man has poor skills, then. I spotted him both at the hospital and in the street.'

'Perhaps he wished to be seen.'

'Because you would warn me…?' Her question wavered into silence. The material in her ugly gown caught the lamplight and one of the ties at her throat was loosened so that the bodice hung away from her skin.

Dipping into his pocket, he brought forth the pendant he had located in a pawnshop two days ago. The look of surprise on her face had him reaching for her gloveless hand. Her skin felt hot and smooth as he placed the bauble within her palm and closed her fingers around it.

'It looked like a family heirloom. I thought perhaps you had lost it?'

A shake of her head brought him the truth. 'I sold it to pay the Davies stables for the rent of their carriage on a Monday. It was my grandmother's.'

Her teeth worried her bottom lip and for just a moment Hawk thought she might begin to cry. But Aurelia St Harlow was thankfully made of sterner stuff.

'You think me a traitor and yet you paid for the restoration of my pendant?'

'I am old enough to realise the world does not deal in only black and white and that grey is a colour subject to much interpretation. I would like to hear how it is you know Delsarte?'

'He was a friend of my husband's. He

came religiously to the parties at Medlands. He is also an opium addict.'

Shocking. He could see it in her face, the crawl of truth and the caution of betrayal.

'Were you at these parties?'

'Once. The first night. Before I understood exactly...'

She did not go on, the silence about them pulsing with intent.

Finally she spoke again. 'It is my opinion that you came to the warehouse in Park Street because you believe there is some illicit business being carried on from those premises. I do not know who sent you there, but it may be prudent on my behalf to suggest we make a deal, my lord. If you could find it in yourself to acknowledge that there is no nefarious activity in my small silk business, I could offer in payment the promise of a letter that would bring to light the truth of your cousin's death.'

'God, Aurelia.'

There was something in what she said that did not make any sense, though he couldn't at this moment fathom quite what it was. Her pulse was hammering in her throat, but she did not give an inch, her gaze full upon him. 'As Charles's cousin I do think you have the right to know the circumstances of his demise and the grey you spoke of a moment ago can be evident even in murder.' Her voice shook and he saw her swallow, her tongue wetting dry lips. Desperately trying to regain given ground, he suspected, and failing.

An ache he had never felt before wound into his chest and shock left him rigid. Was she admitting to both treason and murder? An unexpected tenderness welled within him, enveloping the will to move away.

How did she do this to him so very easily, make him want to protect her and keep her safe? From everyone, even given such damning revelations?

She had as many problems as he did and that was saying something. The very thought made him sad, the isolation of her at complete odds with the words that she uttered. There was no rationality in it, of course, no earthly reason that the attraction between them should shimmer and scorch above Queen and country and justice. But it did, and so brightly that desperation crawled up his arm in shock.

* * *

He wanted her. She could feel the need between them. He wanted her exactly as she wanted him, like an anchor, like a touchstone, like the only person in the whole world who might understand that in tragedy there was sometimes also a glimmer of hope.

For the first time in her life she wondered what might happen were she to put herself first and simply enjoy, but with so many people to protect and so little time to do it she needed to make him understand exactly what she was saying.

'I need immunity from any prosecution, my lord, and you intimated at Hookham's library that you were attracted to me. Perhaps in that we might both find a solution.'

He stepped back, anger on his brow. She noticed how he pulled his jacket from the hanger by the door and shrugged into it, the long tails reaching almost to his shins. He did not want her? He had not been expecting any such admission?

An error! She had made a huge error for the green-gold in his eyes was changed into dangerous amber, any civility still evident simmering under darkness.

'Surely we are adult enough to realise that

the world is often not exactly as it might seem, my lord, and that there are times when the expedience of opportunity might serve us both. I am not an inexperienced green girl, you understand, and you are a man, no doubt, who has enjoyed the company of women.' It was all she could dredge up in the awkward silence, though when he motioned for her to stop she saw that she had lost him.

'The act of loving between a woman and a man is badly done when it is linked so precisely to dishonour, Mrs St Harlow.' His hand shook more than it usually did and he jammed it into his pocket away from notice.

'These might be fine words, Lord Hawkhurst, when one has the choice of exploring different options.' Fury crept into her reply.

'And you think that you do not?'

'I know it.'

'So it is only your body that lies between survival or ruin?'

'Indeed, my sisters might say thus were they to know of your tender.'

Unexpectedly he laughed, the sound echoing about the dark spaces of the room. 'Your sisters? Your father? It is for them that you do this? Who is it that looks out for you,

then, when you have need for some succour?' Now all humour was gone completely.

The question had her turning away because in just those few words he had understood what she had tried so hard to hide.

No one.

She had always been alone. Fighting, trying, hobbling into each successive day with
the weight of the world on her shoulders and
no hope at all of being rid of any of it. Until
his promise of help had thrown her with its
bright and buoyant hope; a golden troth that
had changed everything and now seemed
gone.

She hated how expectation made a mockery of morality and when Stephen Hawkhurst
held her to the spot with a quick grab of her
hand she did her best to shrug him off, short
nails digging into the flesh of his wrist. She
did not try to be careful or gentle. All she
wanted was the cold anger of force, drag-
ging between them, punctuating the impo-
tence and weakness that was her life so far,
never in control.

And now another humiliation, more complete than ever before because even with
such a simple touch she knew that she had
never wanted anyone as much as she wanted

Stephen Hawkhurst. Her right hand slapped hard against his arm as she tried to get away.

He bundled her close in self-defence, holding her fists and tethering her to him. The breath between them mingled, harsh and quick, the warmth of it like a sting.

'I tend to myself.' She would not allow the ease of tears she felt pooling in the back of her eyes. Nay, she writhed at the horror of him seeing such feminine inadequacy, though as his knee came firm between her thighs she understood exactly what she had not before.

He could take her with or without an agreement here in his house at dusk, the solid door shut tight against intrusion and not a soul cognisant of her whereabouts, save a servant who was in his employ. The chaise longue stood just behind them and his glance flicked to the possibility.

'No one looks after you, damn it, Aurelia. Every problem your family has is laid at your doorstep for a solution and another few months of such worries will finish you off. You want to be serviced merely for the chance of your sisters' happiness. You want to give me your body for cold hard cash and an exchange of nothing. Where in that is your satisfaction, or have you played the martyr for so very long you now enjoy the state of suffering Charles made such an art form of?'

He pushed against her, his manhood ripe, the stretch of maleness piercing shock. A dangerous man full of promise and peril. Every part of him was menacing.

'I do not understand...' she began and tipped her face to his, the onslaught of her words stopped by the movement. There was never a chance, she thought later in her room at home, when the memories of the evening returned to leave her sleepless and unsteady, never a chance when a woman like her could have held back the appetite of a lord renowned for getting exactly what he wanted and when he wanted it.

His mouth slid across her own, moulding her face closer with his hands so that the breath he gave her was his, teeth tugging against her lower lip. Pain had its own particular lust after all, she thought, as she pressed forwards to find the promise and the heat.

She knew her bodice was loosened, knew that with only a little effort her breasts could slip from their tether and be in his hands.

And she wanted that, the forbidden avidity which was such a far cry from her work-weary and ordered world.

When would another chance like this one ever arise, the years of her youth stealing by at an ever faster rate and no end in view for any of it? Leaning forwards she let him see exactly what she had on offer and did not look away as his fingers dipped across her throat and came down beneath soft lawn.

Lord, but she was good, the taste of her like some fine wine left in a cellar for years untended and undiscovered, breasts beneath his fingers firm and high and generous. He felt the bodice lower as he tugged at it hard, and then the thin chemise fell away before the warmth of woman was upon him, her nipples rigid, budded and proud.

He was not careful as he pinched such bounty and felt her draw in breath. He was not kind as he broke away from the kiss and covered the gift with his mouth, suckling as he turned tension into compliance.

She was his to take and take, the red whorls of need drawn upon her skin where he had lingered too long, the blood beneath the surface rising heatedly at the pull of his desire. Marked and branded, the porcelain white of her lost into his mounting urgency.

His eyes drank in a beauty beyond comprehension. He felt her hand at his nape keeping him to the task, her breath ragged now and hoarse, passion filling all the cracks of doubt.

'My God.' His voice was shallow, rough, the sound of one who had faltered from some well-worn path and wandered into Heaven.

'My God,' he repeated as he drew back and she made no move at all to hide her wares, but stood there stock-still with her mismatched eyes and her silence.

He could not take her like this, not without all that she should have been accorded and everything she deserved given to her. Her pulse leapt in her throat, her glance dazed and glassy, the stamp of craving drawn in tight rosebud nipples and in the beating want between them.

'Cover yourself.'

She did not move.

'Cover yourself, damn it, Aurelia, before I lose my reason entirely and you understand exactly what it is that you offer so very lightly.'

He picked up her coat and draped it around

her, the dark wool contrasting boldly with the colour of her hair. Like the sirens of Li Galli with their riotous curls ensnaring any man straying upon them as they danced in the deep blue sea of despair.

He had had enough, the pain of his arousal beating hard and unappeased and more than a small share of lust coursing through him. Unsated. The emptiness in him surfaced fully and he could not help his anger.

'Your coat should conceal any damage to your gown and my man will see you home.'

He was relieved when she finally seemed to rouse from her stupor, a dash of anger comforting him. He watched as she turned and fastened the coat across the loosened day dress, tucking her hair into an untidy plait with shaking hands.

Wilson came when he rang, his face devoid of expression as he shepherded her away, her footsteps in the hallway receding into silence.

Gone. Hawk's right hand fisted and the ache in his thigh was more painful than it had been in years. Limping to the fire, he held his palms out to the warmth and hated the way they trembled against the backdrop of flame.

* * *

She sat in the carriage, her back ramrod stiff. His smell was upon her and the depths of shame at her behaviour brought her breath to a standstill. What had she done? Her breasts throbbed under the scratchy wool of her coat, each one remembering the feel of his mouth against her fullness, taking that which she had never before offered to anyone. Closing her eyes, she leant her head back against the cushioned velour feeling… changed. Altered. No longer bound by a frigidity that had defined her.

Her tongue ran across her lips, as if she were asking him back in the darkness, wanting his need to strengthen her. There was nothing left of the girl who had gone to plead the case of her sisters. Now she was only woman.

When a tear traced its way down her cheek she did not wipe it away, but let it fall on to the skin of her hand and be gathered into the fabric below. Her breathing she tempered with a steady rhythm. Two or three more minutes and she would be home and no one must ever know about the events of her lost evening.

She had played her cards and folded. She

doubted Lord Stephen Hawkhurst would ever want to see her or speak with her again.

Stephen listened as his carriage pulled away from the house, his four greys running well. Luc's words came back in the silence. *Only a good woman can get under your skin.* Well, Aurelia St Harlow was neither good nor loyal, her knowledge of Charles's murderer countering all she had told the courts of England and confessed to tonight by some misguided sense of perceived advantage.

Everything they said of her was true. The lies. Her part in her husband's demise. Even the rumour that had circulated about her unusual tastes might have been genuine, given her easy offer of sexual gratification and her attendance at the opium parties of his cousin.

And yet he was still not running to the War Office with the facts at hand and turning her into Shavvon as the traitor he suspected her to be.

Why not? Because underneath everything Aurelia implied he saw the shadows of what was not being said and he had always been adept at understanding nuances. There was something wrong with her confessions, some fact missing that might otherwise explain her actions exactly and he needed to find out just what they were.

For the first time in a long while he capped the bottle he drank from and sat at his desk to write. Lists always worked for him, lists to connect the dots from one to the other and come up with an explanation instead of a mystery.

She was loyal to her family and she was brave. She was hardworking and tenacious. She had been married to his cousin for three long years, yet nobody could remember her in Charles's company because she had never come down to London.

She loved her sisters and she protected her father, and the mother she had spoken of who resided in France was still alive. Could she be as loyal to her? She protected everybody in her family and sheltered them under her wing of refuge, never mind that the task was an onerous and never-ending one. Her money was low and her costs were high and the silks she designed were not yet making ends meet.

A pattern was beginning to form and it was not that of a self-serving mercenary with little regard for the welfare of others.

As more questions formed he jotted them down and, oblivious to the time passing, worked well into the early hours of the morning as he tried to determine the motivation of a woman who was beginning to inhabit his very soul.

Chapter Ten

'But it suits you, Lia, and there is no earthly reason that after eight years away from society you cannot at least show off a few of your charms.'

Leonora's voice crowded in upon doubts as Aurelia looked at herself in the full-length mirror to one end of her sister's room. The emerald gown seemed to glow under the sunlight slanting in from the windows, making her hair look redder and her skin more pale. 'I do not know. It is awfully tight here and very low there.' She pulled at the heavy silk, trying to make the décolletage rise up further over the swell of her breasts.

'It seems low only because you insist on wearing that ghastly high-necked black dress which is a hundred years out of date.'

Her sister's exaggeration made her smile, though a more sobering thought overtook the humour. Perhaps it was time to be the person she should have become before it was too late. For a whole two weeks she had worried as to what might be the outcome of her foolish attempt to bribe Lord Hawkhurst for his continued silence. Every day she had watched for members of the constabulary to come and take her away. Like a sword about to descend. Like walking on eggshells. When exactly would he testify against her and ruin what little reputation she still retained? Lord, perhaps this might be her last chance to wear a gown such as this one.

Shaking her head, she resolved to listen to her sister. The dress had been fashioned by a most respectable seamstress on the advice of Leonora and, with the proper accessories, would hardly be considered 'racy'.

'It's not as if we never receive cards any more, Lia, and Rodney was most insistent that you come with us tonight. Besides, a masked soirée is a perfect opportunity for you to have some fun for you hardly ever go out save to the warehouse and the park with Papa on a Monday. If you tarry too much longer, your chance of anything different will be gone, don't you see, and I want you to be happy.'

Aurelia smiled and when her sister leaned over and kissed her on the cheek she took another quick look at herself. The mask would largely hide her face and if she left before midnight she would have a good chance of remaining anonymous. Hawkhurst would be there—she had heard from Rodney Northrup himself—and it had been that fact that had propelled her headlong into considering putting in an appearance.

She wanted to see Lord Hawkhurst, even from afar. She wanted to be in a room where he was, breathing the same air and seeing the same things that he did because since their contretemps at his town house she had not heard anything at all from him.

The very thought of it made her worry. Should she not cut her losses and simply disappear altogether? A feat more easily accomplished without three sisters all requiring the help of society to find husbands, a very sick father to care for and a business that needed her at the helm for a few months longer.

'Elizabeth Berkeley was in tears last night at the Sorensons'. Lydia Sorenson whipped her away before anyone could enquire what was wrong, but it seems Lord Stephen Hawkhurst might be a part of the problem.'

Breathing in slowly, Aurelia feigned the least bit of interest as she picked at a thread hanging loose from her sleeve. 'In what way?'

'Perhaps he has cried off from offering his hand in marriage. Rodney says his sister Lady Lindsay was never certain about such a match.'

'But Cassandra Lindsay told me Lady Elizabeth was lovely.'

'Lovely for a younger man, perhaps. Lord Hawkhurst needs a woman of more substance and resource.'

The words did not seem the sort Leonora would have normally used. 'Rodney told you that?'

'He did.' She clapped her hands across her mouth. 'Though on reflection he asked me to say nothing of it to anyone and I should have respected his wishes.' She paused for a moment and Aurelia knew that there was something on her mind. 'The thing is…Lord Hawkhurst specifically asked if you were coming tonight. I heard him enquire when he was speaking to Rodney the day before yesterday.'

Despite trying not to, Aurelia reddened and felt the unwelcome glance of her sister's puzzlement upon her. Would he wish to speak to her about Charles? She had promised him a letter, after all, but had not penned it because it was too precarious to entrust such a secret to a man whose motives she did not comprehend. Could the whole evening be a trap?

'Everyone says Lord Hawkhurst is a dangerous man, Lia.'

'I do not need a warning to stay away from him, Leonora, if that is what you fear.'

Her sister frowned. 'There is something about him that reminds me of you.' When Aurelia stayed silent with shock Leonora went on to explain. 'He cares not a whit for the good opinion of others whilst shepherding what little that remains of his family out of the range of any unkindness, and he has a certain menace that is…beguiling. All of the women in society are half in love with him, of course, even given his wildness, but the men admire him, too.'

'Then I cannot see much that is alike between us.'

'He holds secrets and keeps others out.'

'You think that of me?'

'Sometimes I wish you would allow us to help you more. There are things we could do, after all, if only you would let us.'

Turning away, Aurelia nodded. Leonora had grown up over the past few weeks and was no longer the girl she had been. Rodney's influence, she supposed, and was grateful.

'We could help at the warehouse sorting silks and Prudence could do your books. She is most adept at figures, after all, and seldom makes any mistakes. Besides, when I am married to Rodney I can bring the girls out...'

'He has asked you?'

'Not yet, but I think that he will, Lia, I really do.'

An image of herself eight years earlier came to mind. She had told her father of Charles's offer and of her wish to accept it and had been startled by his lack of joy. If only she had listened to his caution and cried off.

'Things will be better, Lia, I know they will be. Soon we will have money to buy the things we need and a proper nurse for Papa. I shall have pin money and servants and a house that is so very beautiful—'

Aurelia stopped her, the frozen ache of her own mistakes marking her next query. 'But would you still love Rodney if he possessed none of these things?'

The smile stayed in her sister's blue eyes. 'Of course I would. If we lived in a tiny cottage with only a single table and two chairs, I should be happy.'

Unlike me, Aurelia thought. So easy to see the stupidity in your own blunders from a distance in time, a hapless eighteen-year-old with the promise of freedom close. Any other suitor would have done her better; a dozen swains and she had taken the one man whose words were empty and whose character was flawed. Decisions held consequences that changed the circumstances of every year that followed. Of all the people in the world she was the one to know this; a wilful debutante who could not be told.

In her mistakes a lack of confidence had crept in; an uncertainty over any choice involving relationships had kept her a prisoner ever since.

At Medlands there had been friends of Charles who had made advances which she had refused—even in London men had come calling. Good men, respected men, men that did not listen to the rumours that swirled about her. But she had never been interested, not even slightly, because as her first freely given choice had been such a mistake it had left her...wary. Yes, that was the exact word. Until Stephen Hawkhurst had kissed her at Taylor's Gap and she had known to the very bottom of her heart that she wanted more.

Fanning her hand, she enjoyed the cold air upon her face. How ironic it was that just when she was beginning to feel in control of her own destiny it might all be taken away.

He knew it was Aurelia St Harlow even from a distance and dressed in a gown that made every other woman in the room pale into insignificance—bright emerald silk, the colour of the sea in the south of France in summer. Her hair this evening was piled into curls, an artful coiffure of living flame, and her lips were full and sensuous beneath the line of the mask.

'Why the hell would Charles's widow wear black for so long when with only a bit of colour she can turn out like that?' Nat's voice held an uncertain admiration.

'Perhaps because she no longer mourns her husband?' Cassie offered and looked directly at Hawkhurst. 'It seems that startling beauty can overcome even a ruined reputation. Word is much of the *ton* has abandoned their dislike of her after the touching show of familial solidarity at your ball.'

'O Fortune, all men call thee fickle…' Hawkhurst recited, watching as a bevy of young and old suitors lined up to speak with Aurelia St Harlow.

'Lady Allum does not look like she has been swayed by public opinion, though is that not her youngest son amongst those awaiting an audience?'

Nathaniel laughed at his wife's remark. 'The sons of half the *ton* seem to be queuing up, and with Mrs St Harlow's charms so generously on display I can see why.' He laughed even more as Cassie swatted her fan across his arm, catching her hand as she did so and bringing it to his lips.

Hawkhurst looked away. Both of his friends had found women who completed them, strong women with their own sense of place and backbone.

Women like Aurelia St Harlow.

Tipping up his glass, he watched her, the ornamental trees placed in careful rows and bedecked in lights, giving his cousin's widow the appearance of an angel held in an unearthly grotto.

He was glad Elizabeth Berkeley and her family were not in attendance, for he did not wish to endure their eyes upon his back. No, tonight in a room of stars and trees and colour he felt the sort of anticipation he couldn't remember sensing for a very long time, the promise of something magical and bewitching. Drawing his mask away from his face, he laid it on the top of his head, pleased for the cold air and freedom.

'Your brother and Leonora Beauchamp seem cosy, Cassie,' Nat said as the young couple swirled by.

'She is a very sweet girl and most loyal to her sister. From general conversation it is said that Mrs St Harlow was virtually a prisoner in your cousin's northern property, Hawk, for all the years of her marriage. Servants talk and the word is Charles was an offhand sort of husband.'

'Offhand?'

'Seldom there. He had other pursuits that kept him occupied, by all accounts'

Shaking his head, Hawkhurst pushed back his hair. 'I was in Europe for much of that time...' He left it there.

'Well, we all knew your cousin had a temper and Alfred said Mrs St Harlow was melancholy. At your ball, remember. He said that it was good to see her happier.'

Biting down on a growing frustration, Hawkhurst hailed a passing waiter. This time he chose a non-alcoholic fruit punch because he had a feeling that he might need all his wits about him in the coming hours and the men around Aurelia St Harlow seemed to be multiplying by the second.

If only she could get away from the crush about her she might be able to stalk Lord Hawkhurst and ask him outright just what action he was going to take. She was sick of all this worrying and the champagne that she had been plied with was also beginning to make her understand exactly what it was that she needed to do.

The dress was uncomfortable, as was the mask. Leonora and Rodney were still dancing and away in the distance she got a small glimpse of Hawkhurst and the Lindsays watching her as if she were a…leper.

Freddy Delsarte was here, too—she had seen him when she had first arrived—though he was nowhere in the numbers of those around her and for that she was grateful. Opening her fan, she made an effort to listen to an earl who stood directly beside her.

'I knew your husband at school, Mrs St Harlow. He was a friend of mine.'

'Indeed.' The warning bells had begun, clanging away in the bottom of her consciousness. This was exactly what it was she did not want: reminders of a past life that was shamefully submissive, reminders of her powerlessness and her compliances.

'If it is a protector you now have a need of—'

She stopped him before he could go further. 'I need nothing from anyone, my lord.' She hated the shake of her voice and the roiling sickness that was beginning to build. She hated the colour of her hair and the way this dress emphasised the curves of her body. She hated that she had come here tonight expecting… She could not name it, though her glance again returned to the tall form of Lord Stephen Hawkhurst.

This was all his fault. If he had taken her at her word and exacted the promises she had given him, all would be settled by now and she would not be standing here surrounded by men who looked her up and down as if she were some delicious morsel to be devoured at will.

Well, she had had enough of it all and if her reputation allowed the gentlemen of the *ton* to act as they were doing here, then it could presumably also work the other way around.

Excusing herself from their company, she opened her fan fully and glided out of the circle of admirers.

She knew he saw her coming, the stillness in him magnified with every step she took as he placed the glass he had just emptied on a table behind him.

'Lady Lindsay, Lord Lindsay.' She gave the words formally because she had no knowledge of whether they would deign to reply, and his name followed. 'Might I have a word in private with you, Lord Hawkhurst?'

Cassandra Lindsay's smile lit up her face and Aurelia felt her tightness ease. 'Indeed, Mrs St Harlow. Why, we were just about to dance, were we not, Nathaniel?'

'Were we? I do not usually…' her husband began, but as his wife's gloved hand gripped his arm he stopped. 'But I suppose if you wish to…'

When they were gone a silence settled, neither comforting nor easy.

'Emerald suits you,' Hawkhurst said unexpectedly after a good amount of time, alluding to the colour of her gown. The edged gold in his eyes was brittle sharp.

'My other dress needed some repair.' She should not have uttered such a thing, of course, but the night in question simmered between them with every step and breath and she could no longer pretend that it had not happened. Besides, two weeks of thinking about what she might or might not say the next time they met had left her strained and tense.

'I will send another gown to replace the one I ruined.'

'No, you will not,' she whispered tightly, glad for the covering of a mask. 'I realise, of course, that things were left unsettled between us, my lord, last time we met. And that the letter I promised has not been sent—'

He stopped her with a movement of his hand.

'Don't write it. There is danger in anything on paper.'

Protection. For her. It was in his eyes as he looked about them. Always checking.

The very knowledge made her move towards him, a shelter amidst turmoil, a refuge from everything that was strange. Here in the very heart of society was a lord who would guard her despite a self-given confession that named her guilty of covering up a crime. She felt the warmth of him against her sleeve in the small place where their arms touched and was glad of it. Just them against the world. What would it feel like if it were a forever thing?

'Delsarte is here tonight.'

'I know. He has not approached me, though.'

'He is dangerous, Aurelia. Dangerous and cunning. You were seen in St Bartholomew's Hospital in his company and that of a French doctor. Touillon, I think is the name.'

'And the British Service knows this?'

'Not yet. I thought to tell you first in the hope that you might offer an explanation.'

'My father is sick, my lord. Doctor Touillon is an expert in the field of elderly mental health.'

'So you visit him without taking the patient?'

For a moment Aurelia longed to tell him everything, to simply open up and tell him all of it here in a crowded room; tell him of her mother's downfall and of Delsarte's threats, tell him of the letters and her dread in delivering them under the cold hard ache of an impossible duty.

Sylvienne. Mama. There was nothing to do but protect her even if it meant sacrificing herself.

'Papa finds travelling anywhere difficult.' The lie was bare on her tongue, the taste of betrayal bitter. The anger in his eyes turned the gold a darker amber.

'I can only protect you to a certain extent, Aurelia. If you cross too many lines, others will be involved…powerful others, too powerful even for me to stop the consequences that will follow.'

When she turned to him, any answer melted away as the promise of masculine sensuality scorched through her. Her whole body throbbed, the twist of delight leaving her momentarily breathless.

He was trying to protect her despite all the odds.

Laying her hand across his arm, she would have said more, but the music about them wound down into silence allowing a passage of people to push their way from the floor.

'I told you that I don't like to dance.' Nathaniel Lindsay's voice held irritation and when Aurelia turned she saw his wife rubbing gingerly at her left foot.

'He won't take lessons. That is the trouble. I have tried and tried to hire a teacher, but he refuses to even consider it.'

Hawkhurst was silent, standing back as Leonora and Rodney completed the group, her sister telling Rodney how she had enjoyed the waltz.

'I was dancing on air, Lia, gliding on a cloud.' Her gaze rested firmly on Northrup, the young man blushing in reply.

Endearing, Aurelia thought, the ardour inside him so honestly expressed. She could not in a million years imagine Hawkhurst showing that sort of embarrassment.

'You went to dance lessons at Eton, Nat. Why did you not progress with them?' Cassandra Lindsay's blue eyes held a wicked twinkle as she addressed her husband, but he did not seem unduly worried by the criticism.

'It wasn't that difficult to feign ill health, and as Mrs Greene, one of the teacher's wives who helped with the dancing, had a soft spot for Hawk and Luc and me she often allowed us to sit it out.'

So Hawkhurst had been schooled at Eton, too? Alongside Nathaniel Lindsay and Lucas Clairmont. She had seen the three of them standing at his ball and talking, the same air of menace and power pervading each of them.

'Hawk was the one who made the most progress even with such little practice. You stood up with him, Mrs St Harlow. Did you float on air?'

Drawing apart instantly, Aurelia saw a look that went between the two men. A look she found hard to interpret because whilst she was certain that Nathaniel Lindsay was teasing her she was also as certain that Stephen Hawkhurst wished that he would not. She was glad Leonora, Rodney and Cassandra were speaking amongst themselves to one side, thus leaving the comment unnoticed.

'Charles told me once that you enjoyed riding?'

'It was a passing phase, my lord.'

'He said that you had a knack that few others possessed. It seems a shame to place little time into such a skill. Now Hawk here has a whole stable full of beauties that I am certain he would be more than willing to share.'

Aurelia knew that the man was setting something up. She could see it in the careful observance that he made of her and in the shifting stance of Lord Hawkhurst, who looked as if he wanted to be anywhere but here.

'My father was a fine horseman before he took to books with such fervour. Now, I tend to help him in the quieter pursuits. Do you read much, my lord?'

The change of subject was deliberate and she was glad when Lindsay took her up on the diversion.

'Never. Hawk does, though. I had heard you met him in Hookham's? Lady Allum brought it to my attention and she intimated your exchange was heated.'

Heated? Aurelia remembered the feel of his tongue on the back of her hand and was about to answer when Lord Hawkhurst suddenly took charge.

'Could you leave us for a moment, Nat? I see George Staples languishing against a pillar beside the band. Go and talk to him?'

The smile on Lord Lindsay's face was broad even with such rudeness, giving Aurelia the impression he had hoped for this outcome all along. 'Be gentle with him, Mrs St Harlow. My friend does not realise yet that a man who plays with fire is liable to be burnt, and badly.' She watched as he bowed and departed.

'Take no notice of St Auburn. Nat is an inveterate snoop and will not rest until he knows the full story behind everything.' He ushered her a little further down the room, to a place where the trees lay behind them and the crush was less noticeable.

'And what is our full story, my lord?' Alone, Aurelia felt braver, their history built up in layers one upon the other and all beginning with the kiss at Taylor's Gap.

'Our story?' He turned the words so that each one of them was carefully pronounced, his eyes grave. 'Our story is unfinished and ill concluded, any hint of what might have been between us buried beneath duty and lies.'

She stood very still.

'Debts of ill repute and payments for silence are things I am trying to rid myself of, Mrs St Harlow, and if the reasons for my cousin's death are going to be pegged to any future problems then I would rather not know of them. For years deception has been my companion, you see, and now I find I need something different altogether.'

'You need honesty?'

The simple question was quietly asked, a pledge that she knew she would never be able to give him with her mother and her father and the faithless arrogance of her dead husband.

'I do.'

Honesty and innocence and pure untainted goodness.

Lady Elizabeth Berkeley.

She suddenly and clearly understood why Lord Hawkhurst had chosen the girl and all hope was lost. A chandelier above them caught the darkness of his hair and the angled planes of his cheeks.

She could not leave it quite at that. 'One person's truth might be another's lies.'

'Nay, integrity is a commodity not so easily bent.'

'Eton taught you that even as you were absconding from your lessons?'

Laughter made the lines on the sides of his eyes wrinkle and those nearest turned round at the sound. Aurelia got the impression that he had not laughed much of late.

'Would you dance with me again, Mrs St Harlow?'

'Yes.' She had heard another waltz strike up, the first chords of Strauss drifting about the room. Aurelia placed her fingers upon his offered arm and they walked on to the floor, the lights dim here and the glow of candles evoking some night-time grotto far from London. She hoped that he would not feel the rapid beat of her heart as he brought her into his arms, closer than she expected, further apart than she wanted.

No one else existed in that room as the music swirled about them and he led her into the steps, the smell of soap and brandy vying for an ascendance, his body hard beneath the superfine in his jacket.

Charles had been softer and heavier and shorter. The very thought made her shiver.

'You are cold?'

'No.' Her eyes met his as she pulled back slightly.

'Was Charles a kind husband, Aurelia?'

'Why do you ask that?' Tonight, in his arms, lying was difficult.

'Cassandra mentioned that you were left alone often and that the servants had talked.'

'I was eighteen and foolish enough to

imagine that marriage to a man I did not know well might solve all the problems in the world.'

'And now you are twenty-six and wise?' His voice was lowered, the husky edge of it inciting all that she remembered from the night in his town house. Hardly strangers. Not quite lovers. There was a danger in it Aurelia found exhilarating and forbidden. Pushing against him so that he might feel the curve of her breasts, she watched his expression change.

Feminine power was surprisingly easy, the potency of her own body something she had never considered before because Charles had left her so very damaged.

'Keep doing that and I will drag you off home before you know what has happened to you and you will not have a chance to change it.'

'Is that a warning, my lord?' Flirtation was another game she had little practice in and she knew he must be able to feel the drum of her heartbeat. Beneath her palm the calm and ordered rhythm of his heart disturbed her. How often a man like him must have been in exactly this position before— a heartsick female flirting to gain an attention she would never be able to win. Such a thought was sobering.

There was no pathway to make the relationship between them different and when the music stopped and the dancers stilled she was glad to move back to where her sister lingered and even more pleased when he made a bow and left her.

Stephen watched Aurelia St Harlow from the other side of the room, trying to get a powerful surge of lust under control and failing. Every part of his body filled with the fury of incomprehension.

'She is a beauty, is she not? Charles's widow?' Nat stood beside him. 'Apart from Cassie and Lilly, the most beautiful female in all of England, would be my guess. She seems alone, though. Substantial and alone. I should not wish to see her hurt further in any way. What is her accent?'

Stephen answered, because to do otherwise would have caused comment. 'French. Her mother was French.'

'Aye, you can see it in the bones of her arms and shoulders. Small like the Anjou princesses. Cassie says that you have looked happier lately, more alive, Hawk. She thinks that the beautiful and mysterious Mrs St Harlow may have something to do with your altered state of affairs.'

'Your wife has a penchant for match-making that has never been successful.' He growled out the words and readjusted the coat-tails of his jacket.

'Well, it has been years since you have courted a woman properly, Stephen, years since you had one that actually counted. Perhaps she is hoping that this time—'

'Stop.' He had bedded a good number of women, but none had made him even consider that any relationship might become permanent save for Elizabeth Berkeley. Her blond curls and blue eyes came to mind, the sweetness in her the thing that had drawn him to her in the first place, but for the past weeks all he had seen in her was extreme youthfulness and an astounding lack of knowledge. When had that happened? When had the fresh goodness of his 'almost fian-cée' become a fault rather than a perfection? He ran a hand across his face and breathed out. Hard.

Ever since meeting Aurelia St Harlow. That's when everything had changed, the

world lost for him in her mismatched eyes
and Titian hair.

He would have to do something about
her—he knew he would—but first he needed
to see the Berkeleys and explain as best as
he could the changed state of his position.

Nathaniel had been right about one thing,
at least. Those who played with fire should
expect to be burnt by it. He winced as the
flames licked at the place he thought his
heart had been long gone from.

The terrace was deserted when Aurelia
managed to escape the throng a good two
hours later. Lord Hawkhurst had danced
with every eligible woman in the room, she
thought…every beautiful, laughing uncomplicated woman, she amended. She wished
he had asked her again, but he hadn't come
near her.

Her feet were sore from her new slippers
and she was tired of looking down and seeing her breasts so easily on display in the
heavy stiffness of emerald silk. She would
not wear such a gown again, no matter what
the inducement, and she hoped that not too
much time would elapse before Leonora indicated that she wished to leave.

Leonora. A few outings had turned her into a woman with as much strength as Emily, her father's youngest sister. Emily Beauchamp had been Aurelia's chaperon in her first Season, a gentle laughing presence and a woman who garnered suitors and admirers, but had never chosen one of them. It was Emily who had introduced her to Charles and who had so favoured the match her father never had. The memory was bittersweet, for her aunt had died of some unexplained illness, here for the day of her wedding and then gone the next. Aurelia had been hauled away by a husband who was impatient to sample all the curves he had found so enticing. The delight she had initially felt at such a barrage of compliments turned into utter despair when she understood that her new groom would not tarry for anyone and that the funeral she hoped to attend was denied to her.

'I do not wish for a wife in black,' Charles had said at the time as he ordered his staff to pack the coach. Running from a house of death was a character trait, but Aurelia had not yet come to understand that about the man she had married, though later she would realise responsibility and familial duty were things to be avoided *at all costs*.

Charles had unlaced her gown so that it looked like one a harlot might have enjoyed wearing, his fingers running under the silk of her skirt even as they sat in the moving carriage. Aye, he enjoyed taking risks and breaking rules, the expected niceties of society angering him, a man who disliked the strict regime of the newly flourishing social moralists. Aurelia had learnt to be careful to hide any criticism for fear of yet another lecture on the mundane, safe and boring pathways she always followed.

She hid everything, she suddenly thought. Her father. Her mother. Her work. Her debts. Her past. Her beating heart when Lord Stephen Hawkhurst came anywhere near her person.

The very concern made her frown and she lifted the mask away. He was as good as engaged to the most beautiful debutante of the Season, a girl lauded for her kindness and her sweet nature. Why, then, did she even imagine that she might be able to catch and hold the eye of a man with more reason than anyone to despise her?

She was twenty-six, for goodness' sake, and eminently sensible, a woman who after The Great Mistake had never made another.

Looking up, she saw that the stars tonight lay between banks of clouds and the temperature was as warm as it ever became in an English summer. The quiet sounds of a fountain further out in the garden made her turn, as she tried to catch a glimpse of water through the darkness.

It was then that she saw him, standing not ten feet away, a cheroot in his hand, the red glow of the tip brightly arcing as he flipped it into the garden.

'Mrs St Harlow.'

He looked less than pleased to see her.

'Lord Hawkhurst.'

Quietly he came closer, careful not to touch, the white in his necktie standing out boldly.

'Do you think that our salvation might lie in formality?' His voice sounded tired and wary, the slur of his words indicating that he had drunk far more than he should have.

'I don't understand.'

'You and I, my lady. Do we skirt around each other forever or do we take a chance and see just where it is this attraction could lead us?'

'You speak in riddles, my lord.' She hated

the forced joviality in her voice, a tone she had so often used with Charles.

'Do I?' He reached out then, and caught her hand, the anger in him felt in even such a small movement. 'The riddle of lust is not so hard to comprehend.' Laying his finger against her wrist, he waited. 'See, it is in your blood tonight, calling me, remembering the other times between us…'

'No.' Her husband had done this, too, pressuring her at the most inopportune of moments, expecting a response, but she was wiser now and older and the horror that blossomed was like a weapon. 'You have had too much to drink, my lord, and your mind is addled.' She threw off his touch, pleased when his hands stayed at his side.

'Not addled, but disappointed. The culmination of a life's work, I suppose, and too little goodness in it.' He tipped his head. 'Are you God-sent, Aurelia? Could you heal the demons that lurk inside me once and for all?'

A different tack. His hands shook more tonight than she had ever seen them do. The wine, perhaps, or the memories?

'I thought you had already refused my prior suggestion of…closeness, Lord Hawkhurst?'

'Those suggestions given without any

form of passion?' He laughed. 'I am not seeking to be a pawn of politics.'

'Then what is it you are after?'

'I only wish I knew.'

The silence lengthened, though it was not difficult or uncomfortable. Wordlessness had its own sort of communication after all, the small turn of a head, the warmth of body heat, the smell of violets and woodsmoke mixed as one.

Finally he spoke again. 'From what I have heard, the state of your union with my cousin was not exactly holy.'

Tonight with all that he knew of her she could no longer skirt around the truth. 'Indeed, our marriage was a mistake.'

'So you killed him?'

In the half-light she saw a tick in the muscle of his jaw, as if he were holding it tense against an answer and the anger in her was as raw as it had been four years ago. 'I cannot deny that I wanted to, though in the end Charles died from his own lack of morals. He brutally raped a pregnant servant and her distraught father made sure that there would be no further…indiscretions. Every woman on the estate probably breathed a little easier that afternoon. I know I did.'

'You told the court this?'

'No. I told them only what it was I had seen.'

'Which was…?'

'I said that my husband had jumped across a poorly constructed barrier whilst exercising his favourite horse and had fallen badly.'

The music inside the ballroom reached them here, soft and lilting against the harsh truth, her candid honesty allowing the sort of relief she could barely believe was possible and even when he remained silent she did not wish to take it back.

'The consideration of any family name is important, do you not think, my lord? I felt that generations of Hawkhursts suffering for the poor judgement of one weak-willed relative was unfair and so I chose to offer another explanation.'

When his eyes darkened she turned to watch the night, hating the way her heart beat so very quickly.

Aurelia St Harlow had allowed herself to be ostracized for years for a crime she had not committed and all in the guise of protection? She was a saint rather than a sinner and if his cousin had materialised out of the darkness then and there he would have killed him himself for everything he had put her through: a court case public and damning and the whispers of her involvement in Charles's demise following her every move.

He remembered the way she had come through the crowd at his ball as the *ton* had given her the cut direct, her chin held high and a smile set on her face. Like a player just before the curtain rises, a certain brittle confidence in her eyes allowing only the glimpse of fright.

'A difficult secret.'

Her small nod in response made him swear.

'And a fiction that has held you a prisoner for years?'

This time she looked at him directly. 'There is no way to refute all that has been said of me and I would countenance no suggestions otherwise. It is not redemption I am searching for, my lord.' Her fingers rose to her neck and he saw that the small diamond pendant he had recovered was back in place. 'Once my sisters are settled into society and I have sold my business I can retire with my father into the very depths of the countryside and I shall never look back.'

The distress in her eyes made his heart

ache. She was like a small and single rose trying to survive through a crack in concrete.

'A sombre ending for a woman who has sacrificed herself for the good of others. If it were me, I should continue on with the colourful gowns and confuse everybody. What more could they say of you, after all?'

Her left hand pulled at the gaping silk of her bodice, trying to close it. 'Once I might not have cared, but now…'

He laughed. 'You are the most fearsome female of my acquaintance, Aurelia. Do not let anyone tell you differently.'

Her smile brought deep dimples to her cheeks. 'I will take that as a compliment, my lord.'

'My cousin never deserved you. He was a man who even as a boy was not easy. He lost his parents just after I lost mine and maybe because of it was damaged. In the end I gave up on trying to know him.'

'Which is why I never saw you at Medlands.'

He shook his head. 'There were other reasons, too.'

'You were in Europe?'

'For a long time.' He smiled.

He wished he could have said more. He
wondered at his cousin's rumoured predilec-
tion for racy women and fast parties. What
had Aurelia seen in a man so untrustworthy
and selfish and why had she married him in
the first place? So many questions to ask and
to answer, hers and his, the worlds they inhabited underpinned by unrevealed confidences.

She had saved him at Taylor's Gap with her
chatter and a kiss that had simply scorched
away any desire to end it all. He might have
jumped if she had not been there, pushing
through a flimsy barrier to a welcomed
oblivion. But instead…

He reached forwards to take a vibrant
red curl with his finger, the silk of it falling
across his palm. 'Then I must thank you for
tending to the Hawkhurst family name as
Charles so obviously did not.'

When she nodded he simply left because
he did not wish to tell her more and because
every part of him wanted to. Gathering his
wits about him, he stepped into the light of
the ballroom and made his way through the
crowded salons to the front portico.

Aurelia closed her eyes and tried to find
her composure. She had told him exactly

what she said she wouldn't and yet relief was the only emotion she could truly identify. Her fingers strayed to her pendant, liking the familiar feel of it.

She had been amazed that he had even remembered the piece, let alone tracked it down and repossessed it. For her.

At the sound of a door opening she took in breath. Had he returned?

'I saw Stephen leave,' Cassandra Lindsay said, 'and he did not look happy. My guess is that you do not, either.' Aurelia saw a question in the other woman's eyes as she turned.

'Nathaniel and I have known Hawk for ever. He is a fine friend and a good man, though for the past six months he has been.... melancholic and pensive.' She stopped and placed her palms across the stone on the top of the terrace wall. Like an anchor. Or a prayer.

Aurelia waited. Sometimes people needed to find their thoughts without interruption.

'We wondered if it was his search for a wife that was making him maudlin. Elizabeth Berkeley is a lovely girl, but she is hardly...strong.'

The word surprised Aurelia. 'Perhaps strength is not what he needs. Perhaps simple, honest and uncomplicated would chase away the demons?'

Cassandra laughed. 'That is what he thinks he needs, but I have had this conversation with my husband many times over and we have come to the conclusion that he needs a woman who can bring him to life again... one who could save him from himself, one who might be able to endure the barriers that he will undoubtedly erect.'

The cliff on Taylor's Gap came to Aurelia's mind. Perhaps he would have pushed further had she not been there?

'Espionage is not an occupation that would leave one much joy, I suspect.'

'You know what he does?' Surprise tempered Cassandra Lindsay's words.

'I have heard rumours.'

Lady Lindsay nodded. 'His brother was killed in France on a mission and Hawk thinks it was his fault that it happened—a personal revenge, if you like, and one that has eaten at his soul. He has seen things that it would be better for a man not to have and without family around him save for Alfred...' She stopped and laid her hand upon Aurelia's. 'Loneliness and responsibility make poor bedfellows. I think you might know that every bit as well as he does, as by all accounts you have had your own battles in life.' She took in a deep breath. 'When I first met Nathaniel I had been a prisoner in France for near on ten months. It was not an easy detention and there were things that happened…things I thought would make Nathaniel seek another more wholesome woman if he knew the truth of it all. I tried to turn him away. I was damaged and I felt I would damage anyone else around me if I let them get close. I ran away on my wedding night to give him the chance of release, but he came after me. He saved me.' She looked Aurelia straight in the eye before she continued. 'If Hawk and you could save each other, any risk might be worth it.'

Then she was gone, sailing back through the door with the grace she'd had coming through it, the honesty and candour left behind her allowing hope. Cassandra Lindsay had not been untouched or unblemished and yet she had risen above adversity and found her place in the world beside a man who would protect her.

Could she do the same?

Her arms curled momentarily around her body and she took in a deep breath before replacing her mask and following Lady Lindsay back into the ballroom.

The anger he was consumed with was nothing like the regrets he now harboured as he thought back to the scene of a few hours ago. Lord, Aurelia had been crucified for the boorish behaviour of her husband and because of it not a word of his cousin's deviousness had ever been uttered.

Unlike her, he cared for little and loved even less. Alfred was in his seventies and might not last for too much longer and when he was gone…there would be nothing of family or blood left. The last Hawkhurst. The final member of a cursed line blotted out by circumstance and sickness and betrayal.

And now even the hope of a faultless, blameless innocent fiancée was lost because he recognised finally what he should have always known. He would ruin Elizabeth Berkeley as surely as she would ruin him, like an apple with one small black spot of rottenness, growing, spreading, consuming flesh that was uncontaminated and pure.

He remembered Aurelia St Harlow's expression on the terrace as she had looked at him, a sort of hope in her eyes. He had wanted to carry her off then and there and bring her home to strip away the emerald gown, claiming all that he could not, spilling his seed into the centre of her womanhood and hoping for…what? A child? An heir? An ending to all the solitude? Even knowing it was wrong, he could not stop the coursing hunger and his cock rose rigid.

His. She would be his. There was no longer any question of it for nothing would stop him. Not duty. Not King. Not country. Not even treason.

'God help us.' He whispered the words into the darkness and closed his eyes against utter need.

Chapter Eleven

The man stepped out in front of her as she
fumbled with the keys on the heavy lock on
the Park Street doorway.

'You are Mrs St Harlow?' The question
was in French.

When she nodded he simply handed her
over a letter.

'She said I was to come back for your answer after you had had a day to look at it.
She said you would give me a reply.'

With that he left. Looking around to see if
anyone else was about and hoping the rapid
beat of her heart might begin to slow, Aurelia let herself in, the unmarked white envelope clutched in her fingers.

She? Could he mean her mother?

Caesar stirred from sleep, stretching and yawning as she untied him and took him outside. Briefly. She wanted to open the note before Kerslake arrived and as an added precaution she snapped the lock behind her when she re-entered the office.

A necklace she recognised as one of her mother's lay wrapped inside a letter. She instantly knew Sylvienne's hand.

Lia
I am ill. Sell this necklace, for I have the need of a maid to help me through this ague. My friend will bring the money back to me and can be trusted.

Grasping the table for balance, Aurelia sat, her fingers straying to the chipped and worn beads of the cut-glass bauble. As cheap and worthless as the life her mother now lived.

She had met Sylvienne again four years ago in Paris on a visit, the untarnished beauty she had once been renowned for slipping into something less attractive, the liberal lifestyle so appealing when she had left England now futile and wretched.

Aurelia, just out of a marriage that smacked of the same sort of despair she saw her mother consumed by, had been desperate to help. Women survived in the only way they knew how and with the roles reversed between them, she felt the need to parent Sylvienne. Even then she had been uneasy with the sort of people her mama had been reduced to dealing with, the crammed and squalid conditions of her rented apartment a far cry from her life in London. No wonder she had become ill. But how ill?

She could not just go to Paris on a whim and leave Papa, not with the silk business on the verge of a good profit and Leonora needing to be chaperoned in the company of Rodney Northrup. Perhaps her mother could be brought to London for some rest and respite? A new worry surfaced. Sylvienne had said again and again she would never live in England, the dreary boredom of it sapping her soul.

Closing her eyes, Aurelia took in a deep breath. Outside bells called true believers to prayer and further afield the shrill blast of a horn sounded, an outgoing vessel on the morning tide making its way to a far-off destination with a full cargo and the hopes of pleasant seas. Ordinary lives. Routine departures. Her own existence seemed beleaguered by stress and unease.

With a flourish she inked her pen and set to writing, the words coming quickly as she decided on the course of action that she would follow. She still had the ruby pin Emily had given her and there were a number of books in the library that her father might not miss. Quick cash. Her fingers crept to the pendant at her neck. She could not pawn this, for Hawkhurst's eyes were everywhere and if he were to find it again…?

Squashing down the rising anger of her thoughts, she locked the envelope in the bottom drawer of her desk and left the warehouse.

'Kerslake is involved. He has been seen in Delsarte's company and they look more than chummy. They were at school together, though they were both expelled for stealing.'

Shavvon looked down at the pile of notes he had on his table and then back up to Hawk. 'What of the woman, Mrs Aurelia St Harlow? What do we know of her?'

'Nothing much.' The lies came easily, falling off Stephen's tongue into the silence of the room. 'She has an old father who is ill and three younger sisters. The Beauchamp silk mills have been in the family for years and she is busy running them.'

Hawk had never once in all of the time he had worked for the British Service omitted a fact that was important to an investigation. Sometimes, when innocents had perished in the quest for a greater good he had hardly turned a hair, reasoning that in any conflict those close to the perpetrators were bound to be damaged and there was little he could do about it.

Yet here he was protecting a woman who had by her own admission omitted salient details to the courts of England about the murder of his cousin. He breathed out in that slow and careful way he had long since perfected, attracting no unwanted attention.

'You know her personally, don't you? Mrs St Harlow, I mean?'

Caution surfaced. 'Vaguely, sir.'

'You met her in the library at Hookham's in Bond Street and then again at the Carringtons' ball yesterday. It seems both times you had long conversations?'

Hawk smiled. He should have realised that he would have been under observation, as well, for trust was a hard commodity to come by in this game. 'She was married to my cousin. It would cause more gossip to give her the cut direct.'

'Then don't. I need you to get closer to the source of these missives and it seems the Park Street warehouse may lead us right to them.'

Again Shavvon noted something on the book before him, a longer observation, this time, and underlined it. 'Watch her carefully. I don't trust her. She has come in front of the courts already and public opinion of her is unflattering.'

Something inside Hawk was breaking as fast as Shavvon was speaking. This would be the last time he would work for the British Service. When he returned he would hand in all correspondence pertaining to intelligence, all the weapons and the charts of countries long at strife with England, all the codes and the books of observances made over thirteen years of spying. It would be finished then, this part of his life, this wandering nothingness that had left him stranded in a place he no longer wished to be.

But first he must warn Aurelia St Harlow that she was being watched and that without due care and diligence she would be dragged in and questioned to within an inch of her life.

Aye, under all the allegiance he felt for the Service another loyalty budded, stronger and more real. He would have liked to have asked what exactly they had on file about her already, but knew that to do so would invite question. So he merely smiled and listened to a diatribe about the inherent dangers of French spies who, according to Shavvon, were crouched like tigers and about to pounce on the very fabric of an unsuspecting British society.

London was as busy as it usually was on a Monday morning just before the luncheon hour. The ruby pin had realised a lot more than Aurelia had thought it would, saving her the task of looking through her father's library for a few tomes that he might not miss.

She noticed Hawkhurst before he did her, crossing the road at Hyde Park Corner. Tattersalls, she thought. The sales it ran were on a Monday, but it was also the day that gamblers received their winnings or were required to pay their debts. Would Stephen Hawkhurst be like Charles in that way, always looking for the next surefire gamble, the easy money that never came? Somehow she doubted it.

'Mrs St Harlow. Are you alone?' The humour she saw in his eyes was unexpected.

'I am, my lord.'

'Then perhaps you might walk with me for a moment. I have something I want to ask of you.'

She stiffened. Was the warehouse in Park Street still being watched? Had Hawkhurst some knowledge of her mother's condition and the need for money? Would he enquire after the Frenchman who had come yesterday, a connection providing him with another way of imagining her disloyalty to the security of the English homelands?

'My Uncle Alfred is celebrating his seventy-fifth birthday tomorrow evening. A quiet dinner party with only the very fewest of guests. He has asked if you might attend.'

The relief felt enormous. 'Of course. I would love to come. Is there some little thing he might want as a present?'

'A good bottle of wine would suit him exactly. He misplaces almost everything else he is given.'

'It is said your uncle was hurt in the Napoleonic campaigns.' She had heard the gossip, of course, much of society losing patience with a man who failed to observe the strict rules of etiquette.

'He took a shot to the head in the second Peninsular campaign under Wellington. That is really the last whole memory he has.'

'It must be difficult to live for so many years without true recall.'

A wobbly cobblestone had her losing her footing and he tucked her hand through his arm.

'Most people's lives are touched by some sort of adversity and in the end it makes them stronger.'

She could not let that pass. 'Sometimes it makes them more afraid.'

'You speak of Charles?'

Unexpectedly she smiled. 'I suppose I do.'

'When did you meet him?'

'In the first weeks of my first Season. He was a fine dancer and he wore his clothes well.'

'Ahh, so shallow, Mrs St Harlow?'

She smiled again, liking the playful tone in his voice. 'You are the only person I have ever admitted such a dreadful nonsense to. In my defence it did not take me long to re- alise that the cut of a man's coat was only a very minor consideration when choosing someone to live the rest of one's life with.'

'And your family? Your father? He approved?'

'Oh, Papa was busy with my stepmother and my sisters and he said my stubbornness reminded him of Mama. It was not a compliment.'

'So you no longer view the state of holy matrimony warmly?'

'I do not.'

He laughed at that, loudly. 'Most women in my company would say the very opposite.'

'Well, you are safe with me, my lord.'

But when the sunlight caught his eyes, softening green into burnished velvet, she knew that she lied to herself, the memory of kisses he had given her making her heart suddenly hum in her chest and the blood of her cheeks rise.

Disengaging her hand, she stepped back. Hawkhurst was a thousand times more dangerous than his cousin had ever been. She just simply wanted to feel what it would be like to wrap her arms around the naked warmth of his skin and allow him…everything.

And there, right in the middle of a crowded

street, with people hurrying by on each side of them, Aurelia understood what it was to truly desire a man. Not any man, but this one: his strength and his goodness, his dangerous solitariness and his secret grief.

Cassandra Lindsay had been right. Elizabeth Berkeley would never understand him as she did, never nurture that part of him that was wild and menacing, never stare into the heart of his solitude and recognise herself in the wasteland.

She looked away.

Something was worrying Aurelia St Harlow, Hawkhurst thought—the talk of marriage, probably, and his roughshod questioning. She had been through hell with his cousin and had made it abundantly clear ever since the first second of meeting at Taylor's Gap that she was not looking for a replacement. Again, he cursed Charles with a vengeance.

'I will send a carriage around just before eight tomorrow night to pick you up.'

He knew finances were tight in Braeburn House.

When she nodded in agreement Hawkhurst made certain he did not tarry longer than he had to in case she thought about the matter and changed her mind.

But as he walked away, the red flame of her hair juxtaposed against the familiar dark of her clothes burnt an image into his brain. And he knew without any doubt that tomorrow night would see an ending to the dance of sensual tension that smouldered between them.

Any thought that it might only be a very small birthday celebration was wiped away as Aurelia started down the hallway behind an austere-looking Hawkhurst servant. Voices of men and women were raised in laughter, though recognising Cassandra Lindsay amongst them she felt a little less worried.

Hawkhurst moved forwards to greet her. 'You look lovely,' he said, his glance taking in the hairstyle she had allowed Leonora to fashion. Normally she bound her hair back, tight against her head to hide the vibrant colour. Tonight she wore it in a looser style, her long curls tied at the nape. She had dispensed completely with the glasses. Her gown was scarlet silk.

Alfred had also risen, a broad smile on his

face. Taking the wrapped present from her reticule, Aurelia handed it to him. The thin lengths of silk in the bow trailed down the side of old thin hands.

Hawkhurst's uncle took his time to look at it, turning it this way and that, the fabric catching the light of a large chandelier above. Finally he loosened the ties and opened the wooden box.

A ring was inside, a ring she had found in a circus years before with her mother, gaudy and substantial, but beautiful, its cut-glass edges showing off all the colours of the rainbow.

'Nothing as mundane as wine, then?' Hawkhurst said this with a tenderness in his tone as his uncle drew the circle on to his finger before leaning across.

'Thank you.' Delight made his eyes sparkle.

'You are most welcome.'

The scar on the side of his head drew the skin around his left eye upwards. Aurelia imagined the pain of receiving such a wound so far away from any hospital and in the middle of a war.

She liked the way Alfred stroked her hand, the expectation and restraints of Victorian society so clearly missing in the uninhibited reaction. She also liked the way Hawkhurst did not hurry him, but waited while his uncle processed what it was he wished to say and do.

The others further away were still chatting as though it was the most normal thing in the world for an elderly gentleman to hold on to her fingers and look deeply into her eyes. Perhaps it was for him, this man lost to time.

'Rings are my favourite jewellery,' he finally said and let her go, walking over to show the others his new and wonderful gift.

'You remembered he liked your pendant?' Hawkhurst asked the question.

'Wine seemed too momentary for a man celebrating the length of seventy-five years.'

'I know he will treasure such a gift. Even the packaging was inspired.'

'Part of Mama's heritage, I think. She was never a woman to do things by halves and I always wrap gifts that way.'

Cassandra rose from her place by the fire to join them.

'Alfred is more than happy, Aurelia. Hawk instructed us to buy wine and we did, but next year we will take your lead and look for something far more original.'

Another woman also walked over, a beautiful, heavily pregnant woman with a white dress embroidered in multicoloured flowers at the neckline. The stitchwork looked like it had been done by a child, the rough sewing out of place against the elegance of the dress.

'I was just telling Hawk, Lilly, that we shall be taking no notice of his suggestions for presents ever again.' There was a soft tone in Cassandra Lindsay's rebuke.

'Absolutely, Mrs St Harlow, for yours has eclipsed our offerings entirely. I am Lillian Clairmont, and my husband is the one trying at this moment to wrestle the ring from Alfred's hand. Lucas's taste in material goods is more than questionable, you see.' She coloured as she realised her criticism. 'But I do not mean to imply that I think your present is…tasteless…' She stopped and shook her head and her hair under the light showed up myriad hues. 'I am expecting our third child very soon and the good manners that used to be the hallmark of my character seem to have all but deserted me.'

As the others laughed, Hawkhurst then made a proper introduction. 'Lillian and Lucas Clairmont are down in London only for a few nights. They have a property in the north and children waiting at home for them.'

'Lucas is the Luc of the dancing lessons at Eton?' Aurelia had suddenly placed him.

'Indeed.' When Clairmont walked to stand beside his wife, Aurelia saw how he wove their fingers together.

'We met at Stephen's ball, Mrs St Harlow. I thought your entrance was one of the grander ones I have seen so far in London, though my first introduction to court may have even eclipsed your own.'

'He arrived brawling with my cousin, blood on his lip and a sneer in his eyes,' Lillian explained with a smile. 'Americans like to…turn up with aplomb, you see.'

'I shall take such information to heart then, Mr Clairmont,' Aurelia returned, 'if I should ever find myself in your homeland.'

'Hawk could bring you. We are due to go back on a holiday next May and I would deem it a pleasure to show you Virginia.'

Surprised by the wash of yearning that was inspired by such an invitation, Aurelia glanced at Stephen Hawkhurst. What would months in each other's company on a boat out of London feel like? Such freedom would be impossible, unless… She shook away the qualifier as all her responsibilities came crashing back in.

This was what her life could have been like had she married wisely. Family, good friends, a man who even in a roomful of others had her heart beating faster, the small flutter at the back of her throat making her swallow.

She wanted Hawkhurst to take her hand and hold it as Lucas Clairmont held his wife's, safety and strength imbued in the very action.

Nathaniel Lindsay broke into her thoughts as he hailed a serving man near and offered up thin glasses of white wine to them all.

'Let's toast to birthdays and friendship,' he said, looking over at Aurelia directly. 'And to marriage,' he added, this time observing Hawkhurst.

Hawkhurst knew what they were trying to do, each one of them, with their hopeful invitations and their clumsy innuendos. After all, he had spent the weeks since his ball fending off questions about Aurelia St Harlow, both Nat and Luc offering advice about his long-term future.

Tonight Aurelia fitted in like a lost glove.

She was not cowed by their teasing—no, far from it, her natural intelligence rising to the jibes with a lively humour and one he had not seen in her before. She fascinated him. She worried him.

This morning a Frenchman had been apprehended outside her warehouse by one of Shavvon's men after he had picked up a package she had given him. Money and silk and a letter to her mother that alluded to more of the same coming the following week.

God. He pushed his hair back and watched her from the old leather wingchair. A deliberate distance. A difficult reminder of all that he had tried to withdraw from.

Deceit. On mismatched eyes and a face that looked as though it belonged to an angel.

He had argued with Shavvon that the contents of the package were nothing like those found in the heavier silk cargo. As a result he had been charged with the task of being Mrs St Harlow's personal minder—a grim and startling assignment given all that he was thinking.

He had hoped his ball could have been the beginning of a new and more innocent life after the fright he had given himself at

Taylor's Gap. And instead, here he was pining for a woman who had more secrets in her eyes than any other he had ever known.

But she fitted here, laughing between Lilly and Cassie and allowing his uncle to hold her hand for an inordinate amount of time after she had given him the present of a ring: a colourful glass ring with the engraving of a dragon through the amber and another on the metal in the band.

Alfred loved her. His friends loved her. He noticed how she thanked each servant every time they offered her something to eat or drink.

Even the damn cat, who more usually scurried away at any slight noise, had sidled up against her on the sofa, purring as her fingers ran through his coat.

The laughter closed in about him, removing such introspection and drawing him out.

'We met at Taylor's Gap,' Aurelia was saying.

'What were you doing down that way, Hawk?' Nat asked the question, a frown on his brow.

Thinking about ending it all, he might have said, but he stayed silent, waiting for her reply.

'He was watching the view—' the edges of her mouth lifted up '—and I was inveigling Lord Hawkhurst into giving my family invitations to his ball.'

'How did you inveigle?' Nat asked this, a wry smile on his face and when Aurelia blushed, Hawkhurst stepped in.

'I was down that way to look over Cloverton's matching greys. The ones you had told me of, Nat.'

'And did they measure up?'

He was pleased with the change of topic. 'They are being delivered next week to Hawthorn Castle. You can come down and see what you think.'

Dinner was a beautiful meal, the French chef presenting two main courses of seafood and chicken along with vegetables, savouries, creamy sauces and a selection of cakes.

Aurelia had been placed next to Lillian and Lucas Clairmont and as far away from Lord Hawkhurst as the table might allow, though looking up once or twice, she found his gaze upon her.

Lillian spoke of her children and of a manor house that they were trying to modernise.

'Hope embroidered the neckline of my

dress,' she said, holding her chest forwards so that it might be viewed properly. 'She is twelve and our oldest.'

'You must have been awfully young, then, when you had her.' Aurelia could not help the comment for Lillian Clairmont barely looked any older than she was.

'Oh, Hope and Charity came to us in a more roundabout fashion. They were always meant to be ours, but it took them a while to find us.'

'Sometimes that happens to people. Take Nat, for example. I found him again in the most unlikely of places.' Cassandra laughed as she spoke.

'Where?' Aurelia began to smile.

'In the bedroom of a run-down boarding house in London. Spying on me.'

'Protecting you, more like.' Nathaniel Lindsay, across the other side of the table, was adamant in his understanding of the situation.

'By insisting that I remove my clothes?'

At Cassie's interjection everyone began to laugh.

It felt so good to be accepted by a company of people who did not judge and who all had their strange quirks and peculiarities. Hawkhurst, however, seemed to remain outside the hilarity, an observer rather than a participant.

Aurelia wanted to sit beside him and take his hand and make him smile as a way of thanking him for asking her tonight. With delicious food in her stomach, a warm cat snuggling across her feet and a group of interesting and genuine people around her, she could not remember ever feeling quite as relaxed.

Much later, after the best evening of her life, she stood with Stephen Hawkhurst and listened to the departing carriages of his friends. Alfred had sought his repose a good few hours earlier and so they were left alone, a dozen candles on a sideboard and not a servant in sight.

Hawkhurst's hand came forwards. 'Stay the night, Aurelia. With me.'

No artifice or pretence. No chance to misunderstand just exactly what he was asking. Just them in a shaded corner of his house, the midnight closing in and the promise of all that had begun at Taylor's Gap sharp upon the air.

She had dreamt of this, imagined such

words in her bedroom late at night, the emptiness inside her calling to be assuaged. But now...now that he had said all that she hoped for, what could it mean?

'If others knew?' She shook her head.

'They won't.'

'Just us, then?' Barely spoken, soft with desire. 'A secret?' The words were out, falling into permission. Her sisters never waited up for her and, if she returned before daylight, only John would know of her absence and he was more than loyal.

At eighteen she had never had a chance, but at twenty-six she did and every fibre of her being wanted to know what it would be like to feel the things that poetry and prose wrote of, the ache that lovers died for, the completeness that overrode armies and philosophers and kings.

If she started this in the way she meant to go on, would there be hope for them beyond the call of duty, diplomacy and expedience? She had made so many mistakes that she was frozen with the fear of making another one and yet...for the first time in her life she knew those things society decreed wrong would be so very right for her.

With a trembling breath she made her

glance meet his, and a belief in herself, badly battered by Charles, began to reform.

Aurelia's mismatched eyes were so damned fine and she had painted her nails red, the colour of lust and of the roses in a vase to one end of the mantel, overblown and wilting.

The heat of her was beguiling, her lips full and beckoning. He had promised to take nothing and yet here she was offering him everything, his blood thundering as if she were naked.

When she lifted her hand to wipe away a tendril of hair he saw she shook, a beam of sudden moonlight at the window turning her hair to scarlet.

The tie at his throat felt too tight and the waistcoat, jacket and trousers heavy against a rising want.

There were so many other things he needed to know about her, but his mind could only concentrate on her form and her smell and on the dimples in her cheeks which deepened with the smallest of movements. He wanted to touch her, wanted to run his hands across the curves and the softness until he knew each and every contour

of her body. But she stopped him with more
words.

'I am not quite as practised in the sensual
arts as you might imagine, Lord Hawkhurst.'

Her admission took him from his reveries
with a startling quickness.

'Charles and I were…distant, you see.'

'How distant?'

'Very. He enjoyed women with more experience than I had.'

'God.'

'I was glad for it.'

His erection rose up another notch, pushing against the superfine of his trousers. He
did not wish to frighten her, but a lust unlike
any he had ever known before caught him
off guard. How did she do this to him, and
so easily? He could not remember one other
woman who had affected him as she did.

Reaching out, he pushed the gown gently off
her shoulders, cupping the bounteous beauty
below the silk.

Heaven. He watched as she flinched at the
feel of him against her nipple, his other hand
moving to her throat and her cheek and tipping her lips to his own.

Home. He was there as his mouth covered
hers and the feel of warm familiar sweet-

ness surrounded him. Deepening the kiss, he pushed inwards, taking all that she would give him and more, force overcoming softness in his need to possess her. Her skin beneath his palms melted like silken liquid, the stain of her red tresses across the paleness sending sense into greater frenzy.

'I want all of you.' The voice sounded nothing like his own, hoarse and desperate, and pulling her hair into a knot, he anchored her close, his other hand around the curve of her bottom.

She let him lift her against his chest, his breath on one cheek and his heartbeat against the other.

'My room is near.'

Up one flight of stairs and then down a short corridor. He carried her as though she were the weight of a feather, though the burden of acquiescence caught solid between them, heavy with suggestion.

When his door shut Aurelia closed her eyes against the four-poster she could see in the corner, and she kept them closed as he lay her down upon the softness, catching breath and counting seconds.

'I would never hurt you, Aurelia.'

She could no longer dwell in her own darkness. 'I know.'

Her scarlet gown was bright against pale coverings and white sheets, and when he removed her shoes and stockings she did not flinch.

His touch strayed to a higher place and she waited for denial or for panic. Neither came, although her breathing worried her. No longer controlled or bridled, the crisp feel of cotton beneath her fingers clasped tightly against an escalating need. When he peeled back her bodice she felt the material fall loosely to her waist, her skirt hitched up to join it.

She felt him look at her, felt his glance know her breasts and her legs and the curved sway of hip, felt how he tethered her with her hair, holding her still, inescapable. Her breath in the silence was ragged, wanting the finesse and the adroitness she knew he would be capable of, wanting the torn-away utterness of what it must be like to be truly loved.

Loved. Her lips curved upwards. He had never said it once and he would not. This was lust and passion and desire on both sides, though the expression in his eyes was one she had not seen there before. Redemption, if she might name it. Her thighs fell open with a will of their own, the hem of scarlet silk cool on burning skin.

He did not hurry. He did not plunge in as Charles would have, caring not a whit for any satisfaction that she needed. Rather he tarried, a small caress here, a longer one there, pressure on a place she had not thought to know, her response surprising as she rose to his ministrations.

A midnight magic.

'Let go, sweetheart,' he whispered as she tensed against ardour. 'Let me take you to a place that is wonderful.'

One finger came inside her, widening the tightness, his other hand flat across her stomach keeping her still. Faster and then faster, his thumb hard against the bud of promise and as she cried out he pressed down, her deep muscles clenched together so that she knew a growing restless wave of release, the ache of it arching her back and making her shout out into the darkness. The keening groan held rapture on its edge.

She was boneless, formless, spent. But she was also elated. She had never felt this pull of seduction, this completeness that took her from this world and far off into a place where all she wanted was more. She no longer cared to be soft or docile or gentle. Finally.

As he brought her fingers to the place his had just left and she felt the wetness, she was mute with the knowledge that her body was not 'dried out and prudish and useless' as Charles had been wont to label her.

The gift was like a treasure.

A single tear traced its way down the side of her cheek.

'Never leave me, Hawk.' She needed to say it, to make him understand. Not just tonight. But for ever.

'I won't.'

When he stood to remove his clothes she watched, the sculptured strength of his body revealed with each discarded garment, though as he took off his trousers Aurelia saw a vivid red scar curling down the whole front of one thigh.

Her finger went out to touch the knotted and raised flesh of a wound beneath each pad.

'Someone has tried to kill you?'

'More "someones" than you could imagine.'

'But not now?'

He only smiled and she understood that whatever took him from England's green and pleasant lands was not finished yet.

She was the most beautiful woman he had ever seen, and he had been with a good number of beautiful women. But it was more than just the physical, Hawkhurst thought.

Aurelia was a woman who had reached out to the ice-cold core of him and begun a thawing. He could feel it inside, the tense hard ache of loneliness dissolving.

She had lived and she had lost and yet still she triumphed and it was this more than anything that made hope rise unbidden. Hers was not the innocent purity of Elizabeth Berkeley which he could have so easily ruined, but another quality that held the kernel of a faith surprisingly and exactly right.

For him.

Like two halves coming together as a whole.

Usually he took women quickly because his life had been bound by danger and by little free time and because he did not wish for the commitment that all of those he had bedded seemed to demand. But this time was different. This time he wanted the night to stretch on for ever, the moon across their skins and a joining connecting body and soul.

Rolling on to her, he opened her thighs with his knee, signalling purpose. She was damp and she was ready, the swollen flesh of her sex calling them together. With one hand under her bottom he raised her up so that the angle of their connection might be more conducive to pleasure and, poised at the opening of her womanhood, he waited.

'I will be gentle,' he promised as he pushed in. She was tight and small and when her eyes widened at the pain he waited until she could accommodate him. Then with one hard and heavy push he was in her, buried to the hilt, her flesh calling in the ancient rhythm of life. Aurelia was his, her hair wrapped like flame about his hand and the generosity of her breasts between them.

The ache of ownership was the most powerful aphrodisiac Hawkhurst had ever experienced and, emptying himself into heat, he gave no thought to protection or hesitation, just need, desperate and all consuming.

He had bruised her, he thought later, with his fingers as he clung to hope and with the drive of his manhood into softness. But she had stiffened as he did, her nails a-tremble on his skin and urging him into a response he could not stop.

The little death, the French called it—the time when a lover died and went to Heaven and back. Joined by sex they moved inwards, straining, wanting the moment to last for ever, listening to each other's heartbeat and knowing each other's breath, the rush of it beaching in relief as wave after wave depleted sanity.

Her fingers strayed, holding the small bud of his nipple, causing Hawk to simply stop breathing.

He would impregnate her; he knew he would, his seed climbing into fertile flesh and growing. He wanted to see the swell of motherhood on her flat pale belly.

Surprise hit him fully as he hardened again, the clenching surge of it taking breath as he turned her against him and pinned her motionless—slowly this time, listening to the rhythms of the long and silvered night. She cried out as his fingers found her desire and brought her with him.

'My Hawk.'

His name, determined and possessive.

Then sleep came, borne upon the wings of exhaustion.

* * *

He woke her as the dawn climbed into the eastern sky, the first flush of pink reminding him of the colour of her skin. He had not slept at all, watching her lie against him, safe and quiet, her hair changing tones as the day bloomed.

'Aurelia. Wake up.'

Blue and brown snapped open. Disorientation. Fear. And then acceptance. He liked the way her fingers curled into his own, a trusting touch.

'It is nearly morning. If others are not to know of this…?' He left the rest unsaid, but already she had risen, her hair falling to her waist as she pulled the bodice up and the creases in her skirts down.

'Your servants?'

He knew what she asked. 'Are asleep still.' He had his own shirt in place by now and his trousers.

'You cannot come with me, Stephen, back to Braeburn House. I need to go alone.'

With her shoes and stockings on and her hair bundled into its more familiar plait, Aurelia looked impatient to be gone.

'My cloak will hide any damage,' he heard her say as they walked back down the stairs, the colour in her cheeks high, but he could not let her go like this. Carefully he took one hand in his own.

'Thank you.'

She smiled then, a full honest humour across her eyes, and allowed him to hold her fingers as they made their way through the front door to hail a hansom cab. After seeing her into it, he stepped back, his figure receding as she was driven the road.

She was home again in her room, the clock only just striking six and not a movement in the house.

Nothing had changed and yet everything had. She was a scarlet woman, a fallen woman, a woman who had seen a chance that she wanted to take and had taken it, in the bed of a lord who had transported her to heaven and back.

Between her thighs was the wetness of their coupling and her lips were swollen. Crossing to her mirror, Aurelia saw how his loving had marked her, branded her, making real that which she might have otherwise thought she imagined.

The scarlet silk highlighted everything.

Her hair. Her pouting mouth. The swell of her bosom where his hands had lingered.

What next? What would happen when she saw Hawk again in the light of day at some soirée with all the manners and expectations of the *ton* swirling about her? What if she saw him in Leonora's presence or in Cassandra's? Would he say something? Would he hold her hand and expect…recognition? Would those about them perceive what she was certain would be in her eyes and on her face, her cursed blushes more prominent now than had been noticeable as a maiden?

She had unstoppered a genie that was both magical and terrible. Lust burnt in her eyes, the glitter of memory having an effect on her stomach and on the places between her legs where he had touched. Throbbing. Craving.

Outside, the first dawn calls of the birds surfaced and the sky was lightening. A new day and a new life. Closing her eyes, she smiled.

Chapter Twelve

Leonora pressed into her side as Rodney Northrup went to find them each a drink.

It had been two days and nights since her…folly? She could conjure up no other way to put it and she had not heard a word from Stephen Hawkhurst since.

'I love these large affairs,' her sister was saying. 'I love the lights and the dresses and the dancing, but most of all I love Rodney.'

Aurelia had to nod in agreement. Cassandra's brother was gracious, charming and attentive. He had called in at Braeburn House almost every morning since Hawkhurst's ball and his composure and temperament had never faltered. 'You are most fortunate to have caught Northrup's eye, Leonora, though I am certain he would say the same about you.'

'You truly like him, Aurelia? I can't tell you just how much that means to me, for I think if he asks me to be his bride I shall say yes.'

Her voice wavered as she looked across the room. 'Is that not Mr James Beauchamp, Lia? I had asked Rodney to point him out to me once and I am certain that is the man speaking with Lord Hawkhurst.'

A tightening in her throat had more to do with the name of Hawkhurst than the mention of a man who would be her father's successor and she felt her fingers grip her reticule with a sudden strength.

'You look pale, Aurelia, but do not worry. All your efforts with Papa have paid off and I have never heard even the slightest of whispers...' She stopped as the two men looked to be coming their way. Three, now, for Nathaniel Lindsay was also at their side.

'Mrs St Harlow, Miss Beauchamp.' Hawkhurst spoke first, the polite smile on his face alluding to none of the secret hours that they had shared in the moonlight. Allowing a good space between them, he introduced James Beauchamp, the mask of cordial social discourse firmly in place.

Her father's heir was nothing like Aurelia had expected. He looked younger, for a start, and was more convivial. Taking her hand warmly, he bowed in respect.

'I had hoped to be introduced to you since my return from the Americas a good three months ago, Mrs St Harlow.'

'Indeed.' She did not look over at Hawkhurst at all. What was he playing at? She had warned him not to interfere and yet here he was and in a venue where she couldn't refuse to at least offer politeness.

Leonora had taken her once-removed cousin's presence much to heart, however, and was impressing upon him the importance of meeting with Harriet and Prudence. Nathaniel Lindsay watched the proceedings with interest.

'We did not see you last evening at the Coopers', Mrs St Harlow. There was a musical interlude and I thought you might have been interested.'

'I had a quiet evening, Lord Lindsay.'

'The influenza is still troubling your father, then?'

Forced into another lie she nodded, catching the hint of humour in Hawkhurst's face. Cassandra had come amongst the group and as a waltz began she ordered Hawkhurst to ask Aurelia to dance before leading her husband on to the floor, James Beauchamp and Leonora following.

When Hawkhurst's arms came about her all she could remember was the wonder of their night together, though she tried her hardest to appear as nonchalant as he was.

'Your nemesis is not a bad chap and as he was pestering Nat for an introduction I thought to do the honours myself. His own abode is supposedly bigger and more prepossessing than Braeburn House.'

'Oh.'

'He is rich, Aurelia, and congenial. In the scheme of things an introduction to one of your sisters might not be too bad a thing— easier than stalking another aristocrat, at least.'

When she did not answer he continued. 'The world is not always crouching to strike, my love.' The unexpected endearment had her looking up. 'Perhaps if you gave it a chance you might end up surprised.'

Of a sudden Aurelia had no real grasp of which issue he spoke on.

'I missed you last night.' He whispered this so that there was no possibility of being overheard.

To one side of the room she noticed Elizabeth Berkeley and her group of friends again dressed mainly in the colour yellow watching them. Danger lurked everywhere here. In Nathaniel Lindsay's humour-filled eyes and in his wife's insistence on Hawk asking her to dance. Even Leonora was taking her place in the unravelling of protections by inviting James Beauchamp home to Braeburn House.

The pursuit of her own needs was causing everything else to fall out of place, invitations, introductions and endearments.

Yet Stephen Hawkhurst had remained honourable in his promise of privacy. Not in a public word or gesture did he appear as a man who had taken all she would offer and wanted to again.

'Are you free tonight?'

She should shake her head and say no. She should smile politely and deem all that had been between them a mistake. She should ask him to release her from any promises and vows whispered in the heat of passion and walk away. Unhurt.

But she couldn't. Instead she waited.

'I will be in the carriage on the corner that turns into Upper Brooke Street at twelve tonight.'

When her heartbeat speeded up she knew that he could feel it. 'Then I shall be there.'

As the music finished Hawkhurst led her back to her sister and Rodney and Cassandra and Nathaniel joined them. As she stood opposite Hawkhurst, making polite conversation, every part of her longed to be closer, knowing him, feeling him.

'You look a little tired, Aurelia.' Cassandra laid a hand on her arm, shaking her back to the present. 'Are you sleeping well of late? I think it must be catching, for Hawk has been exhausted, as well. Yesterday Nathaniel found him asleep after the noon hour when he went to call.' Aurelia did not dare to look over at Stephen Hawkhurst to see his reaction to such a statement, but the web of their lies began to tangle. She knew she would need to be careful and yet she only wished it was already midnight.

His chamber was festooned with candles and freshly cut roses when he led her into it three hours later. A well-thought-out tryst: two glasses and a bottle of wine sat on the table before the sofa. Rhenish, she noticed, and expensive. Her father had once enjoyed it.

'You look beautiful tonight, Aurelia.'

'So do you.'

At that he smiled and, pouring them each a glass, raised his own. 'To us, then. To this. To wherever it takes us.'

His eyes showed a clear-cut want. Not knowing quite know how to reply, she stayed silent.

'Cassandra suspects we are sleeping together.'

'She told you of this.' Her horror vied with sheer embarrassment and that chased on the heels of a worry about Leonora. 'She will never allow Rodney to marry my sister now. I have ruined her chances.'

He laughed at that, then swallowed what was left in his glass. 'I think Cassie's world view may be more expansive than you give her credit for. And she is not a gossipmonger.'

'But someone else will be. One day.'

His hand took hers, all humour gone. 'If that happens, I will protect you.'

But not love you? She almost said it, almost blurted it out, this want for more, because she knew in that one particular moment with the smell of candle wax and petals strangely mixed that she loved Stephen Hawkhurst more than life itself. She would risk her family and the reputation of her sisters for him, throwing all caution to the wind and taking what her body craved.

With trepidation Aurelia walked to the window. She knew Hawkhurst made her foolish and imprudent, but when he moved up behind her she simply turned into his arms and accepted warm lips that came down across her own.

The world reformed into only feeling, his hand across her skirts pulling them up, skin touching skin, his thick maleness scalding her soft flesh, asking for entrance.

'I want you.'

Her voice commanding exactly that which her head had tried to refuse, but the urge was too strong and she gave in to reason as he pushed within her, her nails running down his back in runnels of both shame and passion. But elation had begun to play its high notes deep within, too, the answering need, the thin clenching knowledge that made her back arch as he rode her against the wall in the light of the candles and the moon and the silence.

Afterwards her head dropped on to his shoulders, both their heartbeats racing in unison. And then she began to cry, because she knew she could do nothing to stop this enchantment between them and that it could only end in the ruining of her family.

He felt Aurelia's tears soaking into the fabric of his shirt and listened to the racking sobs.

He had not hurt her physically, he knew that, her body wet and ready for acceptance, her hands and teeth keeping him to his task of loving, and the waves of climax flowing strong between them. When he pulled back he even felt resistance as she tried to halt the uncoupling.

Nothing made sense any more and he struggled for equilibrium.

Aurelia knocked him sideways, that was the trouble. She made him question all that he had believed in and understood to be true.

Every single person he had ever loved had been lost, save for Alfred, and the truth had scalded him with grief. He remembered the master at school giving him the news of his parents' death, unfeelingly, as though death was only a small blink in the day-to-day running of a busy schedule. He remembered his brother, too, gone as he had tried to drag him away from the mad Frenchman on the hills above Lyon.

If you do not love, you can never be hurt.

It had been a motto that he recited every time he left another woman and he had not allowed himself the chance to get close.

Until Aurelia had breached the wall, tearing down his isolation like a wave against a sandcastle, and so easily that any opportunity to regroup was gone.

'I do not want this…this…but I cannot stop it.' Her hands gestured to her body, shaking with the angst of all she relayed to him. Like him, caught in a maelstrom.

'Ahh, sweetheart,' he replied, the endearment coming without notice. 'Believe me when I say this is a gift seldom enjoyed by others.'

'You have felt it before?'

'Never.'

Her answering smile was beautiful. 'I think I should go home now. Papa wakes early sometimes.'

'I will take you.'

* * *

Leonora was waiting in her room as she carefully opened the door and let herself in.

'Where have you been?'

Aurelia knew the moment her sister realised she had been crying. 'What has happened, Lia? Has Hawkhurst hurt you?'

'You saw the carriage?'

'From the window. He is dangerous, Lia. Dangerous and distant and reckless. Rodney says he is a spy.' The look in her sister's eyes nearly broke her heart. 'You cannot do this. You must not. After Charles…'

'He is nothing like his cousin.'

'Hawkhurst has killed people. Lots of them. It is why he carries that darkness within. Oh, my God. You will be ruined again and this time by a master.'

Leonora's glance took in her tousled hair and the creases in the gown.

'You have slept with him?'

Her sister's chest rose in consternation, her mouth falling wide with the shock of it all, but Aurelia found she could not lie.

'More than once.'

'And you will do so again?'

'Yes.'

At the bareness of her reply Leonora sat down. 'Tell me why?'

A different tack and unexpected. No longer a child, but a young woman who needed a reason. 'For years I have been a ruined widow, isolated and alone.' She held up her hand as her sister began to speak. 'Alone in the worrying about our family, trying to piece it together, trying to make it survive and I have never allowed myself to think of anything other than that. Until now.'

'Until Stephen Hawkhurst?'

As she nodded, the next query came. 'Does he love you?'

'It is not love we have spoken of, Leonora, but need. He is thirty-one and I am twenty-six. We are not in the first flush of youth and neither of us is unrealistic.'

'Love is not so proscribed, Lia. I know this now. If he will not make a commitment after all that is between you—'

Aurelia stopped her. 'Then I still would have known how it can be between a man and a woman. When I am old I will have that magic inside.'

'And if there is a child?'

'There will not be.'

'My God, Lia, I have always believed that

you are the strongest woman in the world and now I know it. But even you could be wrong. Please, please be careful.'

When she nodded Leonora hugged her and left, the lamp by her bed flickering in the draught of the door as it closed.

Hawkhurst frightened people. At first he had frightened her, but she had seen beneath the mask he donned in public. A man who thought of flowers and candles to woo her was not as distant as he might profess and the endearments he had whispered as he held her sobbing in the dark after making love were not the actions of an unfeeling and un- caring man.

Neither was the way he worshipped her body.

And if there is a child? Leonora's words came back.

If there was a child she should love it in the same way she loved its father. With all of her body and with all of her heart.

A new beginning.

One hand fell to her stomach, cupping the hope.

Chapter Thirteen

Aurelia took inordinate care with the long lists of numbers before her, balancing this column against that one and rechecking across the rows several times before placing her pen down.

Her bottom lines were being realised, the risks she had taken with fabric lengths and designs, weaves and wefts and colour finally paying off. She could barely believe the profit the company would garner in the next weeks, substantial and open-ended sums of money right down to Christmas. With a flourish she underlined her projected earnings and leaned back.

All the years of work had been worth it. All the doubts and uncertainties and constant gnawing worries had come down to a business that was prosperous and well managed. She allowed herself a quiet glow of pride before laying her pen on the paper and looking out of the window.

The river's presence had encroached on all the buildings around Park Street. Shipbuilders, barge-builders, sailmakers, mastmakers and rope-makers as well as sundry other general shipping-related enterprises had made this area their home.

Sometimes if the wind was right she could smell the Thames, but nearly always she could hear the sounds of it: the horns of passing traders, the shouts of the sailors calling, the flap of canvas and the creak of rope. Her world now, comfortable, known and in its own way exhilarating.

Henry Kerslake returned an hour later and he looked preoccupied and flustered, but the most surprising thing of all was that Frederick Delsarte came in after him.

'You are not welcome here.' She was surprised her voice was so strong.

'As I am your business partner, in the very loose sense of the word, I thought you might be more welcoming.'

When she did not reply he laughed. 'Always the lady. Always the wise voice of reason that Charles was so sick of by the end. Princess Aurelia, with your high-born morals and constant disdain.'

Moving forwards he slapped her, full across the cheek. The force of it made her head snap backwards, her hair falling to her waist in a slow dance of red. Henry Kerslake had gone to stand by the window, looking out. No possible help there. Delsarte's right hand curled into her bosom, outlining the bounty, squeezing hard. 'Stay away from trouble. Stay away from society. But most of all stay away from Lord Stephen Hawkhurst. Do you understand? It may also be prudent for you to think of a reasonable price for the sale of your business.'

Fear made her stiffen. 'It will never be on the market, sir, not to you or any other that might covet it.'

Delsarte kept speaking as though she had said nothing. 'A reasonable sum should see it in my hands, madam. A fair price given the history between us and your straitened circumstances. Kerslake here has a good idea as to how much it is worth and has allowed me to name a starting point.'

Aurelia glanced at Henry, but he did not meet her stare. Rather he looked away as though he wanted no part of this conversation.

'The business is solely in my name, sir. Kerslake has no mandate over any selling price.'

'Take care, then, Mrs St Harlow. Intransigence may only lead to difficulties and with three sisters all needing husbands…' He did not finish.

'Is that a threat?' Caesar pulled against his lead at her tone, straining to get to the newcomer.

'Take it as you will, Aurelia, but a woman of dubious loyalty is likely to do badly when turned over to authorities for questioning. Besides, Hawkhurst has been watching and waiting for you to make a mistake.'

Mentioning the same poor sum he had stated before, Delsarte withdrew, Henry Kerslake disappearing with him and the door shutting behind them to an awful silence.

Sitting down, she took in a breath. Her cheek ached as did her breast. But all she could think of were Delsarte's words.

Hawkhurst has been watching and waiting for you to make a mistake.

The numbers in front of her swam through the tears—small harbingers of a pride that was gone now, drowned in the fear of aloneness.

His skin against hers. The rise of his buttocks as her hands moved across them. The indents on his ribs where bullet holes had punctured and the curling scar upon his thigh. Hawk in the midnight. Magnificent and menacing.

She glanced at the time. Two-thirty in the afternoon. Still hours before she might go to him and be safe. She hated the way she began to shake as her fingers felt the bruised and throbbing skin on her cheek. Dangerous. Isolated. For the first time in a long while Aurelia began to cry.

Someone had hit her. He knew it from the first moment she walked into the hall of his town house, the stain of darkness on her cheek beneath a thick layer of make-up she never wore.

Pulling her into the light, Hawk tipped her chin with his finger so that he might see the damage better. Fury beat at his temples like a drum.

'Who did this to you, Aurelia?'

Her eyes fell away from his. 'Freddy Delsarte.'

'Why?'

'He came to the warehouse today and warned me to stay away from you. He said you were watching me and waiting for a… mistake.' Large tears made a pathway across heavily applied powder.

'I will kill him for this. I swear that I will.'

She caught his hand and held it to her breast. 'Is what he said true, Stephen? Are you watching me?' Now she looked directly at him.

'Yes.'

'Because of Charles?'

'You are being monitored because there have been intelligence codes sent through your silk cargo to France and because known dissenters have been seen in your vicinity.'

'I know nothing of messages in the cargo.' She tried to keep the thoughts of the letters she delivered to Dr Touillon as far as possible from her mind.

'Then I am glad to hear it.'

'My mother is ill and she has sent men to collect some money from me…for a nurse.'

'And Delsarte knows this?'

Politics balanced on the fine edge of intimacy. His question unsteadied her and she knew exactly why Stephen Hawkhurst had been sent to Europe on the government's business. Purpose and resolution defined him, a man of smoke and mirrors, and clever beyond any other she had met.

'Mama lives in Paris and Delsarte intimated that she may be harmed if I do not co-operate.'

'Co-operate? How?'

'Sell my business to him cheaply just as it is beginning to realise profit.'

'And why would you do that? What hold has Frederick Delsarte over you to even consider doing such a thing?'

Aurelia hesitated. The cracks between them would widen with the truth, but there was little that she could do to change that. 'In order to make a living my mother turned to the life of a courtesan and as she got older the clients were less willing to pay quite as much. Sylvienne chose a name that was not her own, but I had visited her and...' She couldn't go on. It was her fault that any of this had happened, after all, and to add injury to insult Freddy Delsarte had become one of her mother's lovers, too. He had told her so at the Hawkhurst ball, implying that he wished to know of her daughter's charms, as well. The very thought of it made her sick.

Webs wove their way around families and the unprotected were left wide open to all sorts of slander. The anger in her surfaced with the shame.

'She is dying of syphilis. I could see it in her face then and now I know it in her words.'

She had never told another soul any of this, but the confession poured out of her, the relief of sharing her darkest fear all encompassing. How often had she kept things bottled up inside and brewing with worry?

It was his strength and his certainty that had brought out such a revelation, a man whose opinions she valued and whose advice she might follow. Years of dealing with each and every problem by herself made her voice shake.

'Shavvon thinks it is you who is implicated in the intelligence sent to France. If we could catch Delsarte and Kerslake instead, you would be freed of it.'

The horror of his revelations had her sitting and Hawkhurst crossed the room, returning with a large glass of brandy.

'Here, drink this. It will help.'

She did as he suggested, the liquor burning at the back of her throat.

Tonight he wore all black, the clothes emphasising the darkness of his hair and the gold in his eyes. The British Service held her name and the address of her family, her sisters and papa. The images of gallows and dark prisons rose in her mind, the rotting flesh of dissidents and murderers in small dank spaces of despair.

She hated the way she was shaking, all the dreams she had fostered disappearing in the comprehension of a reality that held no mind for hope or love. Yet when his arms came around her, drawing her up into his warmth, the cold of the night lessened and business and politics was pushed to one side—just them against the world, the lies and the truths, the good and the bad. Here, for this little time there was a void in judgement, his breath mingling with hers, his fingers tracing patterns on the thin silk of her gown.

'Shhhh, sweetheart, it will be fine, I promise.'

Another troth. Another way that she had made things difficult for him. Did he ever tire of such neediness and how was she to manage if he did?

Her eyes flew open. She could not depend on him like this, not surrender all of her fierceness in a moment of exhaustion. Stephen Hawkhurst had never intimated that their relationship could become permanent, nor did he seek a more public display of affection. She came to him in the dark and she left before the dawn, secrecy clouding all contact.

Tonight, with her cheek aching, Aurelia just wanted to be home. She did not have the defences in place that she had once found simple. No, the barriers she had built for years were shifting as passion refused to be tethered any longer, tumbling through sense and responsibility, tearing away duty and replacing it all with a pure and tantalising desire.

Tears pooled at the back of her eyes and the dull throb on her cheek made everything a hundred times worse, though when he leant down and kissed the edges of the hurt she could not help but smile, feather-light kisses of quiet ease and a great deal of concern.

'If Delsarte touches you again, I will kill him.'

'And spend the rest of your life in prison?'

He laughed at that, but the heat that had

begun to grow took away any thought of
further conversation and when he brought
her down to the woollen rug laid before a
glowing fire she could see in his eyes twin
reflections of flame.

Stephen watched from his window as the
cabriolet drove down the road, taking Aurelia away from him, and he fisted his hands
against his thigh, wishing that he might have
been travelling home with her, seeing her
safe.

Caring for her.

He could barely remember what that felt
like any more and had not known for a long
time, though the deadened anger that had
held him immobile since the death of his
brother wound its way into his throat, quick-
ened, and he swallowed back thickness.

Aurelia. Even her name was beautiful.

If you did not love, you never lost. If you
held people at a distance and took only what
was needed, you could survive.

Flashes of their nights together held him
still, his head tilted towards something he
had missed.

Love. It was not always words that said it.

Love came in the smiles between them

and in the soft honesty at midnight; he could no longer be blind and deaf to all the things Aurelia was saying when she did not speak. Could he love her back in the way she needed? Could he risk a try?

He was glad his hands shook when he looked down because it showed he still had a damn heart inside him. And he knew he would not sleep.

'There is someone here to see you, my lord.' Wilson deposited a card on the bedside table and stood back as Hawk looked at the time on the clock in the corner. Half past ten. He had caught some sleep after all and whatever it was Shavvon wanted it must be important.

'Send him in.'

Alexander Shavvon looked harried and tired and he was barely in the room before he spoke. 'Freddy Delsarte, Henry Kerslake and Mrs St Harlow have gone north. They left an hour ago.'

The whole world slowed around Hawk, a gut-wrenching jerk making his world spin.

'She went willingly?'

'Her servant was found with a lump the

size of Africa on his head and he said she did not.'

Shock held Stephen still.

'They have taken the Great North Road and my guess is they are headed to a manor house Delsarte inherited a year or so ago after winning a game of cards against the Earl of Kendrick. I want to see what Delsarte wants with Mrs St Harlow and what he does. When you know where they are, call in the local constabulary and have Delsarte and Kerslake thrown into gaol and then search the place. Take whomever you want with you.'

Hawk shook his head. 'I'll go alone, sir. It will be easier to remain hidden.'

'Very well. A carriage will be readied. I have already sent people to go into the warehouse to see just what might be discovered there. The family of Mrs St Harlow will need to be told of our concerns, though we will put that off for as long as possible as I do not wish for society to be gossiping about the downfall of suspects we have not yet apprehended.'

Hawk dressed and gathered his coat and hat after Shavvon left and called for his own horse to be brought around. If Delsarte or Kerslake had laid even a finger on Aurelia…

'Focus,' he whispered, 'and help her.'

The building dread clutching at him made his body ache.

Chapter Fourteen

Aurelia's cheek throbbed, the fear inside her making it pound even harder. Delsarte and Kerslake had been waiting for her at the warehouse when she had arrived with John at Park Street this morning and had insisted she accompany them in this carriage. When John had resisted Delsarte had called in other accomplices and they had dragged him away. Aurelia prayed that he had not been hurt too badly.

She had no idea where they were headed, but both men looked angry enough to hurt her if she were to put one foot wrong, and behind them in another coach were the three men she had seen at Park Street.

She prayed that her family would not be

worried out of their wits by her most unchar-
acteristic disappearance when she failed to
arrive home. Her heart sank at the thought
of it.

Straightening her back, she looked ahead,
her bottom teeth grinding against her top
ones. Would Hawkhurst know what had happened? Would he come after her or would
he imagine her involvement to be voluntary
and wash his hands of her altogether?

An inn ahead had Delsarte giving the
driver orders after an hour of travelling.
'Here,' he shouted, the conveyance slowing
to a halt as it pulled into an establishment
that had seen better days. When it stopped
he turned to Aurelia. 'I hope an hour in our
company has persuaded you to be reasonable?'

Waiting till she nodded, he opened the
door and stepped out, making a great fuss
of taking her hand and helping her down
from the conveyance.

Inside was worse than out, the innkeeper
unkempt and leering. Aurelia was glad of
the thick coat she wore as his hand reached
out towards her.

'A beauty, this one, is she not, lads? With
red hair that might burn a man soulless.' A

slurred waft of strong liquor accompanied the insult.

When Delsarte gestured to a table on its own by the window, Aurelia slid into the back pew, her two travelling companions effectively blocking her exit. The others accompanying them sidled across to the bar and ordered a drink.

'What does Hawkhurst know of our operation?' Delsarte asked that question as he lit a cheroot, the smoke of the small thin cigarette dancing between them.

'Nothing. It is me he imagines the traitor because of my mother's nationality.'

'Wrong answer.' Delsarte's voice was low and dangerous. 'He has had us both followed.'

'Then ask him yourself. He is hardly going to discuss his motives with me.'

'You are his lover, Mrs St Harlow, and a woman of much persuasion. I think you could find out exactly what it is you wish to know.'

Aurelia made herself laugh. 'My husband thought me lacking in all ways, sir. Why would his cousin, Lord Hawkhurst, think any differently?'

'You sell yourself short, my dear, and you

always have. Sign the business over to me for the sum mentioned yesterday and I will send you home in the carriage to your family. It all comes down to money in the end, you see, a concept your husband would have entirely understood.'

He waited as the innkeeper deposited two glasses of beer before them and left. 'If I had been called into the witness stand, John Samson would have been sent to gaol for the murder of Charles St Harlow and you, Aurelia St Harlow, for the way you allowed him to get away with it. I was there, you see, watching it all from the house. How easily I could have ruined you.'

The sharp slice of shock had Aurelia's blood pounding—however, she could not afford to just leave his attack there.

'But you didn't speak because you knew Charles was uncontrollable and dangerous and it was a relief that he had finally gone. You didn't speak because the orgies at Medlands would have implicated you and society under the tutelage of Victoria would not have countenanced such depravation. You didn't speak because there were things that had happened at the Yuletide parties at Medlands that would ruin the reputation of any gentleman, yours included.'

'Shut up.' The veins on each side of his temple stood out in a knotted redness and she went quiet. As Delsarte took a good swallow of his drink, the day of Charles's death came back full blown into Aurelia's memory. The blood, the screams, the realisation and the final silence.

She had prayed for years that she might be free of her husband and as Charles had taken his last laboured breath the relief she had felt was indescribable. Murder with strings of temperance and justice attached and a lucky fall for all but Charles. Still the shame of it all made her weary.

'And now with Hawkhurst's untimely questions we have a further problem which is a dangerous thing for us all, Mrs St Harlow. We need cold hard cash to disappear and we are hoping that might come from the sale of your silk business.'

She shook her head. 'There are legal documents to be witnessed and deeds of title to be signed. Such a thing cannot be done on an instant.' She was clutching at straws, she knew, but anything to slow them down and give her time to think would be helpful.

Kerslake brought out a folder from his bag and unfurled all the papers she had just spoken of. 'I have everything we need for the transaction right here, including the right person to buy it.'

And then she understood. They would keep her with them until she signed away her company. Their profit. Their price.

'Do you have a "right person"?'

Delsarte laughed. 'Always the clever one, Mrs St Harlow. Of course we do. A sign of the pen, a tidy profit and a place on the first ship to leave London on the outgoing tide. The simpler the plan, the greater the likelihood of success. Pity we could not have held on to it for longer with the rosy state of your rising sales.'

Everything she had ever worked for gone in the slash of a pen. Her sisters' futures. Her father's comfort. Sylvienne's nurse. She would be thrown upon the debtor's block with the rest of her family, helpless to fight it. Years of endeavour and finally all for nothing. The knife she saw in Delsarte's fist beneath the table had her picking up the pen. While there was life there was hope. Stephen Hawkhurst had at least taught her that.

* * *

The inn came into view after about forty minutes of fast riding. Hawkhurst had checked every stopping place between London and here on the road north and had found no sign of those he sought. The carriage in the stables to one side of the rickety eating house was newly in, the horses being rubbed down by a lad who looked no older than ten.

He flipped the boy a coin. 'Who arrived in this?'

'Two men, sir, and a woman. They are eating inside.'

Another coin followed the first. 'Feed and water my horse and find me another ride.'

'There's only Geordie left, sir.' He pointed to a rundown hack waiting in one end of the barn.

'Then he will have to do. I will be back for my own ride in a few days. Keep him safe.' This time he made sure to offer gold and as the lad bit into it his eyes widened.

'I'll guard your horseflesh with me life, guv. I promise you that.'

Outside, Hawkhurst edged across the yard to look into a door where a number of men were gathered. His eyes searched the room for Delsarte and Aurelia and he saw them almost instantly, an innkeeper leaning over her to look at a document unfurled across the table.

Swearing, he slipped into the shadow of a window that was open, thin and dirty torn lace moving in the rising breeze.

Three others who appeared to be of the same ilk were lined up at the bar. Five opponents. There had been many a time he had battled against more.

Aurelia's back was ramrod straight, the bruise on her cheek today deeper. She had been boxed in against the wall; he saw that immediately and he could only thank God he had found her.

As if she had some premonition that he was somewhere near, her glance swept the room and when he allowed her to find him her mismatched eyes opened wider, both blue and brown not quite believing what they were seeing. He saw her face crumple into fear as he stepped out into the chamber.

Hawkhurst was here, in this very room, and he no longer looked like the man all of society knew, with his careful charm and lofty title. Gone was the lord of manners and means and in his place stood another, the

dangerous edge of him magnified by a pure
and utter menace, the knife fitting his fist
as if he had been born with it and a stillness
that was wild and fierce. She couldn't take
her eyes from the mesmerising transforma-
tion and she knew instinctively he had been
in situations where he had not only saved
lives, but taken them.

He was over at their table before she had
blinked, his fists downing the first man who
tried to stop him in one blow. The second
man was more difficult and he gave fight,
the knife in his hand drawn. Hawkhurst
circled around, crouched, his own weapon
held in a downward fashion, complete con-
centration marking every movement. The
grace of a big man who was neither clumsy
nor awkward, his actions measured in the
sort of purpose only few might achieve. The
shadows in him even at this distance were
marked and she wondered how life had made
a lord born to every luxury such a warrior.
When Hawkhurst arched his knife straight
into the neck of her hapless kidnapper she
looked away.

Death had a face that was all of its own
making and the blank visage of her husband
as he took his final breath came to mind.

Charles had cursed her with the venom she was so used to in his life, but as the blood slowed in his veins she had felt...nothing.

Unlike now, when the quick edge of living had her heart beating with abandon. There were still at least four opponents left. She had no idea how he might stop that many.

Henry Kerslake pulled out a pistol, but Hawkhurst was too quick, the weapon snatched out of his opponent's hand with barely a movement and the butt cracking down upon him. He lay as still as death. Delsarte simply ran, disappearing through the door like a rat down a hole, though the innkeeper looked incensed, the lethal sharpness of a poker from the fire in hand as he advanced upon Hawkhurst.

Scrambling from her seat, Aurelia grabbed the only thing she could find: a large wooden bellows hanging on the wall behind her, its shape edged in steel. She had absolutely no practice in such a defence, but with Hawkhurst's life on the line she was willing to try. The wood crunched down on the skull of the man nearest her.

And then it was over as quickly as it had begun, bodies groaning all over the room as Hawkhurst turned the innkeeper and

Kerslake over to bind them with rope from his pocket. Any sign of the knife was gone, wiped off and secreted away, but as he stood she caught a small grimace of pain. She hoped he was not hurt and her eyes scoured his clothes for a wound, glad when she saw nothing untoward. He had made victory look so very easy she could barely believe any of it had happened, the work of a man who had long been trained in the art of warfare.

Gathering up the papers, Hawkhurst crossed to open the door where a group had formed in the corridor. Other guests, she supposed by their attire, their eyes widened. She heard the whispers of shock as Hawkhurst took the heavy bellows from her and ordered an older man to get a constable.

With her legs wobbling, she sat down upon the nearest seat, fingers threading through the fabric of a cushion. An ancient organza-wrap thread from Italy, she reasoned, given its sheen, and as out of place here as she was. Already she could see questions in Lord Hawkhurst's eyes.

She wanted to get away, wanted to be out into the open and far from a place Delsarte used as a stop-off point. If she had guessed right, there would be some sort of sentry stationed. The innkeeper was one such suspect, his belligerence inciting other questions. The danger of it all was overwhelming.

Forty minutes later they were well on the road, the horse that carried them as run-down as the inn itself.

'We'll need to find some shelter before the storm comes.' Hawkhurst tucked a scratchy grey blanket borrowed from the stables around them both in an effort to generate some warmth as he made this observation, though now that they were out of the range of others Aurelia felt worried for different reasons. He had not spoken at all and she knew that when they stopped there would be things he wished to ask.

The first spots of rain had him pulling the horse off the pathway to gain the cover of heavy bushes and immediately a small open barn not visible from the road could be seen.

He did not push through the shrubs, however, but circled the horse around the edge of them so that twigs were not broken within sight of the highway. Nothing left to chance, no easy clue of their whereabouts. In silence he dismounted and placed his palm flat against the dust of the earth, listening.

To vibration, she supposed, the wind lifting his hair away from the tanned nape at his neck, a man completely in his element amidst nature.

'Do you think anyone will follow?' She kept her voice soft just in case.

'I hope they think us well gone. If we leave before first light and strike north, it will be safer because they will seek us out on the London road.'

'And we won't be there?'

Standing, he reached up to help her off the horse. 'In my experience it is often prudent to do exactly the opposite of what is expected, Aurelia.'

With his hands around her waist he slipped her downwards, the close warmth of contact after fright, beguiling. But there were questions behind the green of his eyes and she knew it was time to be honest with him.

She was pleased, therefore, when he let her go and stood back, for she might not have been able to be so forthcoming had he still touched her.

'Delsarte and Kerslake were at the warehouse when I got there this morning.' Stopping, she breathed, once and then twice before continuing. 'My mother is French,

as you know, but there are other things I
have not said.'

He waited.

Aurelia wished her voice did not waver
as it did, and she swallowed hard. 'I told
you once before that I went to visit Mama
after Charles had died. I think people got the
wrong impression about what I was doing
there.'

'How?'

'They thought I was wealthy and black-
mailed me to send money for the protection
of my mother.'

'And what of the letters you delivered to
Dr Touillon?'

She hated the way she blushed, for she
could feel the colour washing across her
cheeks in a red bloom of shame.

'You know about those?' So it was true,
all that they said of Stephen Hawkhurst. He
was a part of the British Service and she had
been caught like a small mouse in a very
large trap. Her heart began to hammer, fast
and then faster.

'Intelligence has its own channels. With
just a little effort you could be thrown into
gaol and after taking into account your history...' He let the rest slide.

'I did not know what was inside the letters.'

This time his laughter had an edge to it that was more distant. 'The law cares not a jot for perceived innocence, Aurelia, for it deals only in cold hard facts. You delivered information from France to one known in England for sedition and libel and good people will have suffered.'

Because his line in the sand was drawn so differently from her own she could barely voice their new understanding. 'So after rescuing me from one fate you will deliver me into another?'

'No, damn it. I am here to save you from yourself and in doing so we may both be sacrificed.'

His reply came like a dousing of icy cold water. 'Why?'

'God only knows, for I don't,' he returned and walked to the far edge of the shelter, both hands fisted by his side as if wrestling with a problem far greater than even the one he admitted. 'You could be a traitor, and you are a liar. You had some hand in killing my cousin, and the man you work with, Henry Kerslake, is a known dissident. Yet here I am, running from a further group of them in an effort to keep you safe.' He stopped and tipped his head into the wind, holding his hand to silence any reply, as horse hooves came in fast from the south.

She held her breath in sheer and utter fright. If Hawkhurst was killed as he tried to protect her...

No. She would not think like this. Her whole mind simply went into a slow-motion numbness as the reality of everything settled.

'The wind and the rain will help,' he whispered and led her to the horse, placing his hands around its muzzle. 'Get on.'

Waiting until she was seated, he led the mount from the barn, the rain now falling in heavy spots and cold. She was glad of her coat and her thick winter boots, though still a shivering crept in, making her choke with trepidation.

The field they walked across was uneven, rutted and dark, the half-moon behind a heavy bank of clouds allowing an untracked escape that its fuller counterpart might not have. She wished she had a hat, for the water dripped down the neck of her coat and across her face in a constant runnel.

Nothing human stirred in the darkness

though, only the branches of trees swaying
wild with the gathering breeze, a heavy scattering of wind-torn leaves in the air around
them. Then the sound of gunfire was close,
red raw flame exploding across her head,
the light against darkness blinding. She felt
the sharp sting of it and then the answering flash of steel thrown across darkness,
Hawkhurst's knife rifling into a solid out-
line not ten feet away. A man she recognised
from the inn. He fell slowly down on to the
newly ploughed field, simply folding in on
himself as he went, surprise lost in death.

In the silence Hawkhurst walked away to
reclaim both his weapon and the gun, tucking them into the belt at his waist as he returned.

'He was alone. Are you all right?'

Her hand crept to the pain at her shoulder.
Had she been shot? There wasn't blood and
she could find no place where the coat had
torn. Perhaps it was only a muscle sore from
the unfamiliar gait of a horse?

When she nodded Hawkhurst began to
move, glancing at the sky the few times that
the moon appeared as if it were a signpost
to the way he sought. She wondered why he
did not mount and ride behind her, though

the answer was in the breath of the horse, more and more strained with every passing moment.

The night wore on until they came across a country lane and he relaxed into an easier pace, the limp of his right leg easily seen in the oncoming dawn.

Hawkhurst knew this place, the line of trees down the road and the row of houses braced to the wind. He had been here many times in the past few years and the anger that had consumed him began to thaw a little with this sweet promise of safety.

They were out of harm's way for now. Even the rain seemed to have abated as the first light of a new day streamed into darkness.

'This is Luc and Lilly's house. We will be safe here.'

The gate to Woodruff Abbey was as prepossessing as the house and Hawkhurst was pleased that any stragglers tracking them would have second thoughts in going further. Glancing at Aurelia, he saw that she looked tired, the white pallor of her skin alarming. The fact that she had delved into things she never should have was secondary to getting her into a hot bath and clothes that were not sodden.

'I hope no one has followed?'

Her voice was small, hesitant, the antithesis of all she had seemed in town. She had drawn into herself somehow, her arms plastered to her side and any interest in her surroundings long gone.

The house came into view, Lillian's touch everywhere, her sense of style on the architecture and in the gardens unerring and understated, transforming the formerly dishevelled and abandoned place into a home.

Aurelia had the same love of beautiful things with her silks and her fabric squares of many hues. He could hear the admiration in her voice as she spoke. 'I have never seen…a white-and-green garden before.' The whole of one side of the driveway was planted in specimens that displayed all the hues of pale whilst on the other side reds, oranges and purples vied for attention.

Hawkhurst hoped like hell that Luc was up from London.

She felt sick and nauseous, the ordered beauty of the Abbey such a stark contrast to the way her own life was turning out. Stephen Hawkhurst was angry again and the pain in her shoulder had not abated.

All the colour, movement and noise confused her and tears slipped down her cheek. She wiped them away quickly, though she thought Hawkhurst might have seen this, as his frown deepened.

When the door opened Lillian came forwards, her dress the colour of her pale plants and two children by her side. Lucas Clairmont was there, too, a frown on his brow as the day began to spin. Clutching the reins tighter, she swallowed and tried to smile, though her lips seemed dry and tight. She was glad she was not standing and that up here on this old and tired horse she was out of the way of such fervent greetings. An onlooker, watching the warm reunion of good friends. She could not even begin to think of the energy it would take to dismount. A puppy had wandered over and was jumping up at her boots, though a blonde child with the bluest eyes shooed him down, her hands waving him away.

'He is new, our puppy, and he has bad manners sometimes. Mama says he will learn, but Hope and I think he will always be naughty.' Deep dimples graced her cheeks, giving Aurelia the impression that she rather hoped this might be so.

Hawkhurst had come to her side, too, and looked at her quizzically. 'Can I help you down?'

She only smiled and shook her head, for the task of lifting herself from this horse was just suddenly too big and too difficult. If she could stay here up above the world, she might be all right, watching others, observing life. Her own seemed to be ebbing away somehow beneath each breath, images of her past flashing strangely before her. Nothing mattered any more. She was here and safe with Hawkhurst and he was happy. She could see it in his eyes and in his smile, his good friends surrounding him and in a place that looked like something from a fairy tale.

And then he was moving towards her, his humour changing to concern as his hands reached out. The puppy barked, a high shrill sound, and the child shouted as the day whirled into chaos.

Closing her eyes, she simply let everything recede and centred on breathing. It was the only thing that she could still do!

* * *

Aurelia was as pale as he had ever seen her, her eyes glazed and distant, a small indrawn statue on a tired horse, fingers clutching the reins with desperation as she began to sway.

Alarm made Hawkhurst reach up, the feel of her skin cold against his own as she collapsed against his chest. The realisation of something else sticky and warm had him turning her carefully and he saw his coat was stained with blood from where she had settled. Howling out her name, he walked in haste to the blue salon at the right of the main door and placed her down on the large sofa. Luc and Lillian followed in his wake.

Aurelia was dying, he knew that she was, each breath more shallow than the last. He tore at her coat and the buttons pinged on to the floor as the garment drooped across her shoulders.

'Here.' The blue dress had a hole in it and blood oozed out through the damaged fabric in a steady stream. Unsheathing his knife, he deftly cut the material away and swore.

She'd been shot. The gunfire in the field close and loud, searing the darkness with red. And she had said nothing. God, for the first time in a life of espionage and battle he panicked, heeling the palm of his hand into the artery that fed the blood flow with a shaking uncertainty and hating the possibilities that flew into his mind.

Luc's touch across his shoulder was the only thing still tethering him to sanity. 'Our physician is coming, Stephen, and in my experience wounds like this can look far worse than they are.'

Lillian had taken the children away, but she returned now, her face as worried as her husband's.

'How was she hurt?'

'It was my fault. I should have known they would follow. I should have kept her safe.'

Blue eyes scanned his face and he could hide nothing, the raw grief of worry eliciting a rare swearword from a woman who seldom broke any rules at all. And then she, too, was beside him, a long thin piece of fabric in her hand which she wound tight around Aurelia's upper arm, her pale white dress splashed in red.

'We won't let her die, Stephen, and the bleeding is slowing. Look.'

The oozing had ceased a little, but as he calculated the time and volume lost since being shot, it was of little comfort. He had seen people bleed out before his eyes a number of times and they were always cold, like Aurelia was.

He merely nodded. With her bruised cheek and her wet hair loosened vibrant red against such utter paleness of skin, Aurelia had the look of a mermaid washed up on some foreign beach. Alone and forsaken. All Hawkhurst wanted to do was to hold her, keep her close, but as the doctor hurried in carrying a bag he stood back instead, allowing the man access.

'She is lucky,' the physician said finally after a thorough examination of her arm. 'The bullet passed through and has ruptured nothing. There is a substantial blood loss, of course, from all the movement, and she will be weak. But she is young and healthy so a full recuperation should occur.' His hand rested across her forehead before measuring the rate of pulse in the artery of her neck.

'She will need someone with her tonight in case she becomes feverish. If you could carry her upstairs, Lord Hawkhurst, to one of the bedchambers, I will dress the wound there.'

'The pink room, I think, Hawk,' Lillian

said as he lifted her. 'There is a generous basin in the alcove and a sofa by the window.' She laid her hand against his and he was pleased for a contact that was warm and well meant.

The lack of luggage had not yet been mentioned, nor had Luc and Lillian plied him with questions about the obvious attack but he could tell Luc was keen to know if danger was still imminent.

He hoped like hell that he had not been tracked to this place, but he prayed even harder that Aurelia would feel a lot better by the morning.

And beneath everything there simmered the problem of how he could protect her from the long and all-knowing arm of the British Service in general and Alexander Shavvon in particular, a man who must now be wondering where on earth it was they had gone to ground.

Chapter Fifteen

The flicker of a candle was the first thing she saw, a tiny orange flame that sent light across a beautiful room swathed in dusky pink.

Hawkhurst was there, stretched out on a chair near her bed, his legs crossed and his head bent at an awkward angle. Turning to look at him, she felt pain sear through her arm, the heat of sickness making her weak. Blood still lingered on the sleeve of his shirt, indicating that he had neither changed his clothes nor bathed. She could barely swallow, so dry was her throat. 'Water?'

He came fully awake as she breathed the word, raising her head to the rim of a cup and allowing small sips before taking it back. 'How do you feel?'

Aurelia did not know, for a violent headache had scattered all logic, leaving her floundering somewhat in a place that was frightening. 'S-scared.'

'You will live.' The words were strong and assured, no doubts within them. If he left, she was suddenly certain that she would never survive this.

'Stay?'

He simply took her uninjured hand into his and brought her fingers to his lips. Feeling the scratchiness of his unshaved face and the warmth of his touch, she closed her eyes.

I love you. The honesty of the thought brought her peace as a single tear traced its way down the side of her eye and fell into her hair spread across the pillow. Fear subsided, too, her world narrowed to this one room. Pink. Like a young girl's, the silk in long curtains of the finest quality and the furniture harking back to an older and more generous time.

In the distance she could hear the first dawn call of birds.

'It will be morning soon,' Hawk said as he saw her listening, his eyes softer now, threads of relief through tired, worn gold. He did not let go of her hand.

'Where are we?' She found it difficult to remember things.

'Woodruff Abbey. Luc and Lillian's country home.' His voice was slow and quiet, and speaking of something other than sickness calmed her. If she was truly dying, would he be so unhurried?

'Is it safe?'

'Yes.' A wealth of trust lay in the word. Delsarte and the implications of espionage and deceit crouched further away in another time and place, a conversation that could keep until she felt stronger. In London her family would be frantic—she knew they would be—but right now she needed to think of herself.

She smiled. No longer all alone. Closing her eyes against hope, she slept.

'Delsarte should be shot for this.'

'He will be.'

'And Aurelia St Harlow? What will happen to her?'

Stephen stood against the balustrade, looking over a garden to one side of the bedroom. 'The injury is only a small part of Aurelia's worries, Luc, for if Shavvon has got wind of her involvement with the French intelligence then I cannot think of a single way to save her.'

No, that was not quite true. Hawkhurst shook his head at the thought, for there was one. If he married her here and now, his name might be enough protection.

Luc seemed to be veering down the same track. 'Shavvon owes you, Stephen, and if you brought in Delsarte and any of his group still left, surely that could be an end to it.'

'Perhaps.' The Atherton title was an old and venerable one and peers of the realm and their families were seldom dragged before the courts. Besides, under law, presumptive legal unity treated husband and wife as one and he could fight far better than Aurelia would ever be able to.

'Lilly thinks she has had enough hurt in her life and now needs safeguarding.'

Anger solidified. If Woodruff Abbey was beautiful, then Atherton was doubly so and the luxury and ease of the place might soften all the hard edges of the obstacles between them. He could help her, if she would let him, and in return…

She was nothing like Elizabeth Berkeley and all the other young ladies who had set their caps at his wealth or titles. She did not want baubles and dresses, the newest of carriages or the largest of diamonds. He could not imagine her lolling around the *ton*, collecting gossip or enjoying scandal. Lord, she had been the centre of some of the most damning slander of all and seen first-hand the hurt it caused and the suffering.

She had harboured the father of a girl badly used by Charles and taken the criticism upon her own head for years and years. No, Aurelia was nothing like any other he had ever encountered and for that fact he was grateful. She was her very own person, solid and worthy. Someone like that at his side would be...formidable. He smiled at the thought.

The doctor had indicated she should be well enough to travel by the end of the week and before that he had a job to do. With Delsarte locked up and the sorry saga of the Park Street warehouse finished, he would be in a stronger position to help her entirely.

But first he would employ guards to watch the Abbey while he was away, just in case Delsarte had obtained some knowledge of their movements.

Lillian Clairmont was one of the most beautiful women Aurelia had ever seen, with her pale eyes, unmarked skin and her remarkable sense of fashion. Today she wore a gown that was a warm peach, a diversion from the paler tones she had worn across the past days and the hue sat against her skin well. Aurelia wondered how the gold silk from the fine looms of Macclesfield might look upon her and decided she would send her a bolt as a thank-you gift as soon as she had returned to London. Hawkhurst had grabbed the documents pertaining to the business before leaving the inn and they were tucked safely away and little worse for wear. She would make certain the deeds were placed in her safe once they were back at Braeburn House.

They? She frowned.

Hawkhurst was no longer here. She knew this because Lillian had said so yesterday in a passing conversation, and it had been four days since he had sat with her in the dark hours before dawn and held her hand. She refrained from asking if he would return, understanding in the ruckus with Delsarte and the letters passed to Touillon that he might never wish to see her again.

The hurt of it stung even more than the bullet hole.

'I thought today you would wish to have a bath. My maid could wash your hair and you could get dressed and sit outside in the garden in the sunshine. The pink peonies are out and so are the white irises.'

Aurelia thought of her gown ruined by the shooting. With no other clothes save a coat in about the same condition she doubted she would be able to be 'dressed' at all.

She was about to decline the opportunity when a maid sailed through into the room carrying a dress of pale cream in one arm and the matching slippers and shawl in the other.

'My husband is always saying that I have far too many clothes so you would be doing me a great favour if you took a few off my hands. Why, with a little help we will have you looking most presentable again.'

The kindness in her tone was disarming. 'The doyennes of London society might warn you away should you ask of my character, Mrs Clairmont, and believe me there are many who would feel your assistance to be both unwarranted and unwise.'

Hawkhurst's friend's wife merely laughed. 'Luc taught me to follow my heart and I have quite decided to do just that.'

Thickness obstructed Aurelia's throat as she looked away. Lillian Clairmont had the same sort of graciousness that Cassandra Lindsay did and both had been more than kind. She wished that they could have been good friends, their lives playing out across the years like the characters in the books she read in her father's library. For ever linked and loyal. But under the circumstances it was not fiction that she should be fostering.

'I have a bullet through my arm for a reason and there are things I have done that I should not have.'

'Well, Alfred likes you.'

'Pardon?' Aurelia suddenly couldn't understand quite where this conversation was leading.

'Stephen's uncle. He thinks you are the answer to his prayers and has been extolling your charms to all and sundry. He says that you think of everybody save yourself and that it is high time someone took you in hand and worried for you.'

'Someone?'

'Hawk, I am guessing.' She began to giggle and because the whole thing was just so ridiculous Aurelia did, too.

It felt so good to laugh, to let the worry

and fear spill out into something different altogether here in a beautiful room in the early afternoon sunshine with a full vase of roses on her mantel.

Orange roses. The way they clashed with the paler hues of the room was surprising.

Lillian surprised her, too, as she leant over and laid her fingers across the top of her uninjured arm. 'Stephen needs to be happy again and I think you are just the person to make him so.'

'He thinks I am a traitor.'

'And are you?'

'No.'

'Well, then, make him realise exactly who you are. He has been alone all of his life and seconded to a job that has taken his soul bit by bit. He used to laugh more. It would be so good to find him such again.'

The words sobered Aurelia's joy because laughter had been as foreign to her across the last eight years as it had been to him. Still, she remembered a time when joy had filled her up with an optimism that Charles had completely negated.

'Thank you for taking me in and for...' Her hands shook as she encompassed the room with a gesture, and to her horror, tears gathered and fell. 'I do not usually cry,' she managed, as the beautiful Lillian Clairmont sat on the bed beside her and gathered her in, careful not to touch the thick bandage.

'Then I am glad you feel able to do so with me.'

Her perfume was one of flowers fresh blooming and Aurelia's more normal reticence was replaced by a want to explain. 'My mother is in Paris and the man who shot at me was part of a group who had made threats against her safety. I was trying to save her, but now I think I have made everything immeasurably worse.'

'Sometimes the way forwards is not as straight and easy as you might like it to be, but there are those who can help you if you let them.'

'If it is Stephen that you speak of, he has left already and I do not know how to tell him any of it.'

'He has gone to find Delsarte and will be back as soon as he has.'

'Oh.' Aurelia sat up in bed and swung her legs across the side, for a clean bath and a new gown suddenly seemed like a very good idea.

Delsarte had slid into a hole like the rat that he was and was nowhere to be found.

Hawk hoped he might have left England alto-gether, though a feeling down his spine told him he hadn't. But with the rains slanting in from the north the byways had become quagmires and any tracks able to be followed had been swallowed up by mud.

Scanning the heavens above him, he rounded the final hills down into Wood-ruff Abbey. A storm darkened the sky, a rainbow sliding into the last prisms of day-light. The house in the folds of ash trees was beautiful though he wished it might have been Atherton standing there before him, its gilded cream turrets and thick crenellated walls calling him home as no other place had ever been able to manage.

It had been so long since he had been back, the memories of a family taken from him by sickness leaving him unwilling to return; until now, until this moment, until the vision of Aurelia St Harlow gracing the gardens and the salons and his bedroom can-celled out everything before it.

'God.' He whispered the word into the night and urged his mount onwards, the shadows of the Abbey beckoning. Aurel-ia's curtains were drawn. He realised that as he counted the windows along the second floor and above the portico. Had her wound worsened? Had the fever returned? Had the doctor's advice been as sage as he hoped it would be? His fingers tightened on the reins and he frowned at such an unfamiliar anxiety.

It was then that he saw her, walking through the gardens on the western side of the house, the formal box hedges obscuring her before she came through the canopied archways of greenness to wait beside the driveway. She wore a dress of Lilly's, he thought, cream silk bright through the oncoming darkness. Her hair was almost loose, caught in an untidy knot at the back of her head so that tendrils fell from it, curling Titian against pale. Her left arm was held immobile against her chest by a skilfully fashioned sling, the tie of it made into a bow.

'You are well, Lord Hawkhurst?' Her eyes slid across his body, checking as she asked the question.

'Delsarte eluded me, though I have an idea as to where he will go to next.' If she felt relief, she did not show it, her face carefully schooled into a smile that gave away nothing.

'When Lucas Clairmont returned yes-

terday and you didn't I thought perhaps...'
For the first time she faltered, stopping as
she swallowed before beginning again. 'I
thought you might have gone back to London.'

'But you watched for my return anyway?'

She looked back at the manor house, hesitation taking her away a step and then bringing her back. 'I should not wish for you to be hurt because of my actions.'

'The missives you delivered to Touillon were a decoy to the real work undertaken by Delsarte, the silk samples allowing an easy passage of intelligence. Kerslake has confessed to everything for the chance of a pardon.' He hoped she did not understand what these words implied. 'Sometimes it is prudent to sacrifice the freedom of one for the capture of many.'

'Including me?'

He turned away because he could see in her eyes exactly what he knew would be reflected in his own.

'The people you work for are now looking for me?' She had reasoned it out anyway, the fright on her face escalated to panic.

'There is another way.'

'What way?'

'I can marry you.' He wished he had put more emotion into the words before he said them. 'My family name might see you safe.'

'No.'

'There is no choice, Aurelia, for treason holds a harsh punishment.'

She shook her head hard. 'Marriage to a man with no mind to want you is a similar penance, Lord Hawkhurst.'

'You speak of Charles?'

Caught in stillness the cream of her gown was bathed in a shimmering gold.

Lord Stephen Hawkhurst would marry her because of duty and danger. He would link his name to hers in protection and shelter only, nothing at all mentioned of love.

Treason? They could try her for that? They already had the word of Kerslake, his liberation depending upon the scope of his confession. Henry wouldn't be kind. She knew it. He would throw her into a light that would not be flattering because in doing so he heightened his own chances of deliverance.

She hated the way her heart was beating, all the dreams she had fostered disappearing in the comprehension of a reality that held no mind for hope or love. It was worse because of it, this altered understanding— a proclamation given without any of the intended promise.

'I do not think you understand the gravity of your predicament or the speed with which the British Service might act upon it.'

'But you will tell me?'

'They know where you are and unless we leave immediately I will have no hope to stop them from transporting you south to face charges. Atherton is the only option of protection left.'

'Atherton?' She could not understand what he meant in her moment of panic.

'My title and my house. It takes a lot more work to hang a member of the peerage's wife.'

Pragmatic and utilitarian. Her mouth felt dry at the notion of such a loveless union— history repeating itself.

Worse and worse. The words drove into her heart like the spar she had seen embedded in the chest of Charles.

Love me, Hawk, she longed to whisper. *Love me in the same way that I love you and even should I die tomorrow it would all be worth it.*

But she could see nothing in his eyes save the need to be gone as he took her by the arm and led her towards the house, his pace hurried. Lucas Clairmont met them at the front door, and after a quick conversation with Stephen he sent a servant to find a thick winter coat that she recognised as one of his wife's.

It was over, and all she could do was to follow Stephen out to the Abbey stables and allow him to help her into a carriage readied with a basket of food on one seat and two heavy blankets on the other.

Chapter Sixteen

Aurelia remembered back to the only other time she had come to Atherton with Charles just after she had been married. With its ornate turrets reaching upwards from a three-storey façade it was a sight to see. Cream stone glinted in the late afternoon sun, giving the impression of a castle of light. A manicured park fell down to a pond, many bridges crossing the wandering waterways, a vista of beauty that stretched far out into the middle distance.

The thick crenellated walls of Atherton must have been a fortress once and it was not hard to imagine the Hawkhurst ancestors ranging across the parapets and warding off the sieges of some troublesome enemy.

Like they still might be now. Hawkhurst had been mindful all the way across the countryside, checking, waiting in the smaller tracks whilst scanning the road for those who might be following them.

'Is it safe?'

She asked the question because she did not wish to be the serpent bringing trouble into Eden.

'Very.' No hesitation in his answer as he looked at the billowing flags of the ancient Hawkhurst seat, the charge of the black hawk standing out before a golden chevron and etched into a field of the lightest blue.

Generations of Hawkhursts had fought beneath these banners, dying for causes so much more noble than her own. She wondered what Hawkhurst might be feeling, as he had made little effort in conversation, and in his eyes she noticed a thread of an irritation that was dispiriting.

Did he wonder as to why he had brought her here? Was he wishing to be back in London with the beautiful Lady Elizabeth Berkeley, her goodness and pure innocence such that he should never have to chase across half of England with a group of thugs on his tail as he was with her?

The arrival of servants at the front door brought her attention back to the moment, maid after maid and man after man lining up along the pebbled circular driveway. When the steps of the conveyance were pulled down they both descended. Stephen did not touch her again.

'Simpson.' Hawk brought out his hand to the man who stepped forward and held the others warmly. 'This is Mrs St Harlow, my wife-to-be.'

Shock held Aurelia immobile as a shimmer of recognition passed wordlessly down the long line of servants. The St Harlow name would hardly be salubrious and Charles's early demise must have been a topic of conversation for months in the downstairs chambers of the castle. Besides, the idea of marriage mooted privately between themselves was very different from a direct proclamation to all who might listen.

Her shoulder ached as did her cheek and this charade was the very last thing she felt like being a part of. Still, with the long reach of the law, she knew that to insist otherwise and in front of so many people would be unwise.

Finally they were in the house and in a

room to one side of the wide and lavishly furnished front hall. As the door closed against the last departing maid there was a moment's silence and Aurelia wished that instead of looking so fierce Hawkhurst would simply walk forwards to take her in his arms to kiss her.

It might fix everything, a kiss: her worry, her fear, her aching uncertainty of walking into yet another mistaken marriage.

'The vicar from the Atherton chapel will wed us first thing in the morning.'

'Without banns?'

'That will be taken care of.' His voice was flat and weary.

'If there is any other way that I might find protection, then I think we should consider—' He stopped her.

'There is not, Aurelia.'

Looking down at the cream dress Lillian had bequeathed her, Aurelia saw how the hours of being on the road had rumpled the silk. Hawk looked no better, his jacket dirty and his trousers and boots dusty.

'I am sure that our union will be viewed very badly by all who hear of it.' She tried to keep the shaking from her voice.

'Then let us hope we can keep it secret for

a while longer. I have worked for the British Service for over a decade and the least that they could accord me from this fiasco is the right of a few weeks of silence.'

A fiasco. She wondered if he might hear the sound of her heart breaking into a hundred little pieces even as she mulled over her options.

'Annulments are not viewed favourably and are complex and difficult to procure. I could not afford the money needed for one.'

'Enough, Aurelia.' His hand came down across his thigh hard and dust spun into the late evening air, the motes swirling in the last slant of sun.

He said her name in a way that made her look up, the implied protection surprising, and suddenly she was breathless. Could he mean to help her because he wanted her, needed her, in the same way that she needed him? Hope blossomed with a fervour that she tried her hardest to hide.

Mismatched eyes held the sort of wariness he so often saw in her. She did not wish to marry him, that much was certain, but even in the face of such strident opposition he could not be kind. He would drag her to the altar voiceless if he needed to and the vicar had been in his employ long enough to understand the implications of ruin for a woman.

He would prevail because he was the Lord of Atherton and because the tithes he paid to the church were generous and frequent. He would insist on the ceremony because without it Aurelia St Harlow would be lost to the vagaries of law.

'The family chapel is just through here.'

Aurelia took in a breath. She had slept right through the night and felt more able to cope with everything this morning. On waking she had found the dress borrowed from Lillian hanging before the wardrobe, carefully cleaned and pressed. She left the sling on the chair.

As Hawkhurst opened a set of double doors behind him, Aurelia saw the polished brown wood of pews with their velvet inlays and prayer books neatly stacked in front. The ceiling was vaulted and the windows were drawn in lead and coloured glass, the Christ child on Mary's knee, His head garlanded in flowers.

Standing at the top of the aisle was an old

clergyman, whitened eyebrows and hair attesting to an age well reached.

'I will begin when you are ready, my lord.' He rearranged a few papers on the pulpit before him.

Hawkhurst did not even look at her as he bade her forwards and Aurelia felt as though she had stepped into a travesty she could not stop, the parts of a marriage laid out in a cold-blooded fashion and only for the reason of pretence.

'I do not think...'

The minister stopped momentarily to observe her, his piercing eyes daring her to speak further. 'You are a child of God and as such you deserve the sanctity of a union which is the most joyous of all His celebrations.'

Joyous? She remembered her last wedding with a shudder. Field flowers now waved their heads in a vase on a table and a number of the servants of Atherton had filed in behind her to sit quietly.

Witnesses.

The contrast to her marriage to Charles with all its pomp and circumstance could not have been greater.

Already an organ had begun to play, soft

music filling the chapel, the only thing that was beautiful. The lump in her throat thickened at the purity of the notes.

He wished his uncle could have been here, standing beside him, or Lucas or Nathaniel, but there was nobody save the rows of servants, hair tidied and hands washed. His mouth was dry and the blisters on both palms from long days of riding stung with the salt of sweat.

His marriage day—his first and his last. He wanted to lean over and take Aurelia's hand in his own and hold it tight in an effort to tell her that all was not lost and that although she felt the farce of it keenly, to him it was...*perfect*.

The very word made him smile. Perfect implied a consent that was without compromise. Perfect implied compliance and sanction and a God-given need of the union they were about to enter into. Perfect presupposed a sense of history behind them that had reached up to this moment. The frown on his bride-to-be's face etched a heavy line into her forehead, negating any such acquiescence.

'We are here today to join this man and

this woman in holy matrimony.' Johnathon Cattrell's voice was low and even, the pledge of for ever well formed. When Stephen glanced down he saw that every knuckle on Aurelia's hands was stretched white.

His parents had been married here and his grandparents and all the other Hawkhursts before him. He felt the rightness of it settle in his bones.

Protection was only a tiny part of why he was standing here. He knew that with a blinding honesty. When the minister asked for a ring he drew the Atherton signet from his own hand. The circle of gold was far too big, but it was all he had. Aurelia could not offer any token, but Johnathon Cattrell ignored such an omission in the face of everything else that was strange.

Then it was finished. Man and wife. For ever.

He took her hand and she did not pull away. The smiling, clapping servants followed them out.

The wedding breakfast was sumptuous, the top table in the room flanked by at least ten others, the same wild flowers she had seen in the chapel in vases on each one.

Every manner of meat sat on large plates

carved into succulent-looking pieces, plus vegetables, fruits, sauces, shellfish, savouries and a selection of iced cakes.

Large jugs of wine and smaller ones of orange water were scattered between the food. The glasses were all crystal and the plates a fine white china.

When Hawkhurst stood as they were all seated a hush came over the room.

'Welcome to Atherton, Lady Hawkhurst. I hope you might come to love this place as much as I do and that all the years of our life here will be happy ones.' Raising his glass, he offered a toast. 'To Lady Aurelia, the most beautiful bride any man could want.'

Her name echoed across the room, and in the eyes of those around her she saw a genuine and warm welcome. Sipping at the wine, she felt herself relax. *The most beautiful bride any man could want.* Not tarnished, second-hand and a traitor? Not a woman he had had to marry under duress because of politics?

She had not seen Stephen in a setting like this before, surrounded by his workers and staff. Here, he did not seem so much the lord, but a part of a great estate that required much co-operation and respect. She wondered how many other men of London society could have made the transition so easily.

She also thought of the time after the feast, the time when they would be alone. A rush of heat fanned through her body, fierce and possessive, and when she felt his arm against her own she did not move away, but stayed still, enjoying the tiny contact.

Her husband. Her lover. For ever. She took one sip of wine and then another.

Aurelia was leaning against him and he liked the feel of her beside him. Today there was something different about her, some quieter acceptance that was seen in her eyes and in her laughter. Mrs Simpson was regaling her with various accounts of family life when he had been a child and his wife was listening with intent.

A new beginning for Atherton. Another chance at normal.

'Did you have brothers and sisters yourself when you were growing up, my lady?' He could hear the interest in his housekeeper's voice.

'Not really. My half-sisters are much younger than I am, you see, and my mother had left.'

'Then you'll be needing a large family here to take away the loneliness.'

The laughter accompanying this remark brought a blush to Aurelia's cheeks and Stephen stepped in. Perhaps now was a good time for them to withdraw. Already the tables were becoming rowdier, the treat of a holiday and good food having their effect.

The room was Hawkhurst's. She could tell it was from the books and the writing desk and a wardrobe with clothes that looked exactly his size.

'I have not stayed here much over the last years so the room is full of things from the past.'

She crossed to a globe on the table, the brass holder it sat in carved with the figure of a dragon.

'Like this?'

Aurelia spun the countries around, the colours of oceans, lands and rivers melding into one.

He laughed. 'I always found travel fascinating. If you look closer, you will see the marks on all the lands I wished to visit.'

'And have you?'

'Most of them.'

'And what about the pocket watch?'

'It was my brother's. I never wound it again after he died.'

'"Time moves on in good ways and in bad." Mama used to say that to me.' She looked at him then, his neckcloth loosened and the gold in his eyes velvet. 'I wish I had not been married before. I wish this was my very first time and that…and that…we had met back then, when I was younger. You would have liked me more.'

He laughed again.

In the mirror opposite she caught sight of herself, her colour heightened and her eyes glittering. She looked so similar to the girls Charles had brought to Medlands in the first year of their marriage, his wild and unbridled parties demanding the sort of feminine willingness that was palpable in the expressions of those attending.

Thank goodness she was not back there, moving like a ghost around the few rooms left to her use, always frightened and never certain.

This relationship could not be like before, with Charles. She could not endure another loveless and distant marriage in which both parties had dealt with each other in hatred and mistrust. This one had to be different, better, real.

Shaking her head, she chastised herself for such fantasy. It was duty and obligation that had brought each of them to this pass. Fluffy oversized cushions on the bed behind beckoned and a carafe of wine and two glasses sat on a cabinet nearby.

There would be expectations placed on the head of the title, and one of them resulting from a marriage even as hasty and ill-conceived as this one would be children. Heirs to trace the name of Hawkhurst down through the centuries and link them to the ancestors who had already been. Antiquity lived in a castle like Atherton and no one person's needs were bigger than the narrative of history. Especially not hers.

With Charles she had withdrawn from any intimacy as soon as she realised what sort of man he was. But here…here a different truth lingered.

'You sell yourself too short, my lady. A wife with a blameless slate would not suit me at all. Oh, granted, once I thought so, but now…'

The compliment made her cheeks redden and she knew the blush of it was showing on her face. She hoped he might step forwards and show her exactly what it meant to be his wife. The dampness between her legs throbbed, the lust of want so familiar she felt dizzy from it.

She wanted him, wanted him in the same way they had wanted each other in London, breathless and burning, wrapped in each other's arms until the morning. As Hawk poured two glasses of the red wine, she tried to take stock of everything.

'To us,' he said, handing her a goblet, careful not to touch her as he moved back and drank. His eyes did not stray from her own.

Drink took the edge from panic and she needed it to. Her nipples hardened in a movement that sent small clenches of need to her core as he touched her arm.

'Does it hurt?'

Shaking her head, she smiled. 'Mrs Simpson found a bandage this morning and she dressed it. The ointment took away any pain.'

He placed her left hand in his. 'I will find you a ring that fits as soon as I can. My mother had many and...'

His words petered out as she placed her lips on his fingers, one by one.

'I love you, Stephen.'

There was nothing else to say to a man who had never given up on her, even when he thought her a traitor.

He shook his head at her proclamation and tried to move back, but she would not let him. 'Ahhh, sweetheart, you don't know who I am inside,' he said, his free hand above his heart as if shielding some dark thing that he did not wish her to see. 'And if you did...'

'Then I would love you more.' She could not allow his distance to break honesty into pieces. He could not love her back in the way that she wanted, he could not say the words that she could barely hold back each and every time she was with him.

I love you.

I love you with every breath and every heartbeat.

'It is the imperfections that make people interesting, Stephen, those things that are hidden from everybody else.'

'I have killed people, Aurelia, many people.'

'In the name of a country trying to keep its citizens safe. England should thank you for it.'

'If only it were so simple.' Yearning lay in his voice.

'Sometimes it is, my love,' she returned. 'Sometimes to forget for a moment is simple.' Her fingers began to unbutton his jacket and she was pleased as he allowed her to slip it off. His neckcloth, waistcoat and shirt followed. He breathed in quickly as he traced the line of bandage across her left arm and helped her out of Lillian's gown.

'If you had not survived it…' His thumb crossed her left breast, drawing a name. His name. Hawk. She read it in the quiet touch of skin.

Her husband. Joined by God and by law. Contentment gave way to alarm, though, as his fingers passed over raised skin at her nape and he pushed her hair aside.

'What happened here?' It was not the mark a lady should have had, she knew this, the quick slice of Charles's knife a warning to comply.

'I married your cousin on a whim and he soon regretted it.' She took a deep breath. 'He was my husband and I had promised before God to obey him. If I had given him his marriage rights perhaps none of what happened would have happened. John's daughter might have had her baby and would still have been alive.'

Hawkhurst shook his head. 'A man who would slice the skin of the neck of his wife is an unbalanced and dangerous one, Aurelia. You were wise to stay clear of him and there is no shame in protecting yourself.'

She smiled at that. 'As you protected your brother?'

Shock ran through him. 'Who told you?'

'Lillian did. She said the scar on your thigh was from your effort to save your brother when he was caught in the crossfire of war.'

'It was a fumbled effort. He died in my arms.'

Lord, he could give out advice, but he could not receive it. The irony of that made him smile and when she began again to talk he made himself listen.

'Both of us have been scarred by death then, it seems, and have paid the price. Perhaps you were right when you said that it is time for the guilt to end, you with your brother and me with Charles.'

Her fingers strayed and she held the small bud of his nipple between them, causing Hawk to simply stop breathing.

Would there ever come a time when he did not want to possess her? Laving his tongue at her throat, he left a mark, reddened by passion, and took her to the marriage bed.

* * *

It was night when he woke, the moon full through the windows, its pale shadows lighting the limbs of Lady Aurelia Hawkhurst. Hawkhurst repeated the name to himself, liking the way it tripped from his tongue into the silence, midnight long since passed.

Her head was on his chest and her arms were thrown out across him, the ring he had placed there easily seen in the moonlight on her fingers. Further off the breeze rattled the leaves on the giant oaks that marched along the driveway.

Atherton and Aurelia. The rightness of it made him smile and he lay still just in case she might wake and see all that she meant to him.

Why did he not tell her? Why did he not give her back the words she had given to him all across the long and lovely day?

Treasure.

'It can be simple,' she had said. But he knew that it never was.

Chapter Seventeen

〰️

Hawkhurst was gone when she awoke next, the sun streaming into the room.

Mrs Simpson came in with a quick knock, her face wreathed in smiles and a basin of steaming hot water in her hands.

'I'm to help you wash, my lady, and then dress.'

Aurelia felt a wash of embarrassment rise up across her face. The bed was in a state and, quickly drawing up the blanket from the base, she tried to hide some of the wreckage.

'A successful wedding night needs to show some…shambles,' the sensible and eminently practical Mrs Simpson declared. 'In my experience if it does not then there is not much hope for a future happiness.'

'You are married?'

'For thirty-five years, my lady, and to a man I love as much now as I did when I married him.'

Such chatter calmed Aurelia. 'Does Lord Hawkhurst come to Atherton often?' she asked.

'Not so often. When he was a child he lived here with his parents, but they passed on with a sickness and he has not returned for great lengths of time since.'

The information was horrifying. She imagined the hurt and the loneliness of a young Stephen, his world fallen to pieces.

'This is why Lord Hawkhurst is a rolling stone, I'd be thinking, though a good marriage might change that.'

'Thank you for telling me.'

'But come, my lady, your new husband is waiting for you in the downstairs breakfast room.'

Stephen stood by the window in the blue salon and looked out across the long green lawns. Once he had played here with his brother, laughing and shouting as they ran and fished and climbed. His parents had stayed at Atherton for most of the year, want-

ing the quiet and the beauty of the place, but
it had been the same isolation that had even-
tually killed them—too far for any doctor to
come with a bag of tricks and a cure.

They had been buried together in the
small family graveyard and Daniel and he
had been brought up from school to observe
the solemn and joyless process.

He wiped his hair away from his eyes.
Now he was back with a woman who was
nothing like the bride he had thought to take,
and where did that leave him? Smitten and
ensnared in the promise of all that she was,
that was where.

To wake up this morning with her lying
beside him and watch the trust and peace on
her face had been a revelation. He was no
longer just beholden to himself and he hated
this power she held over him, no will of his
own save the need to empty his lust inside
her like a green boy in the first flush of ado-
lescence. He abhorred the thought, too, that
if anything ever happened to her he might
not survive it. Would not survive it.

It had been the same with his parents
all those years ago when the news of their
deaths had left him breathless and crouched

against the side of a cold brick building struggling for the air that he could not take.

If Aurelia left him… He shook his head and put away the thought, but the possibility of pregnancy loomed large and he knew the percentages of healthy women who never made it through labour. Everything was dangerous when a person wriggled through the careful guard of indifference and slid into the heart. It was why he had even considered offering for Elizabeth Berkeley because he knew that there was a part of him that she could never have touched.

Unlike Aurelia.

He swallowed and thought of his mother. Catherine would have liked his new wife, for they had the same sort of independence and cleverness. His father would have liked her, too, with her wide-ranging knowledge of politics and opinions.

A noise at the door made him turn and there she was before him, a shawl that he recognised as one of his mother's tucked around her shoulders, the softer shade of pink setting off the fiery colour of her hair. She wore it just as his mother had, tucked up in a loose knot at her nape.

The circles of life spun in ways that were

fathomless and incomprehensible and perhaps after all it was just as simple as Aurelia had said it was. Signalling to the waiting footman to begin serving breakfast, he helped his bride into a seat at the table.

He was dressed in country clothes this morning, the fabric in his jacket and his trousers fine tweed and beautifully tailored. On her part Aurelia could barely meet his glance as she pondered over their hours in a bedchamber filled with delight. Today in the company of servants tending to them and the formality of a lordly seat overshadowing everything, a sort of hesitant uncertainty hovered.

She could not believe that this distant lord was the very same man who had kissed her into oblivion and given of his body so freely.

'I would like to show you Atherton today on horseback, if you feel up to it.'

Just the thought of a jaunt outside raised her spirits. 'My arm is a lot better and even if it tires I am well able to manage one-handed.'

'Good. Mrs Simpson will find one of my mother's riding habits for you to wear. It will be of the old style, of course, but I think you would be much the same size. Would eleven o'clock suit you?'

'That sounds lovely.' The toast was dry in her mouth as she bit into it. So formal and stilted. She wished he would look at her as he had in the moonlight, passion in his eyes as need for her filled him. Today it was as if she could have been anyone.

'The people who work on Atherton would no doubt enjoy a word or two with their new mistress if you would not be averse to stopping.'

'Indeed I would not be averse to such a thing.'

His eyes creased at her answer, puzzlement lurking, and because of it she smiled. Quick wariness took his glance away and he made much of buttering his toast before lifting up a jug of freshly squeezed and sweetened lemon juice to fill a fluted glass—the business of an ordinary breakfast underpinned by a night of high passion and lust.

If she had been braver, she would have reached out and placed her hand over his and asked him if they might again repair to their bedroom to speak in a language that needed no words at all. If she had known that his feelings for her were as strong as the ones she held for him, she would have done just that, but she had no such certainty. And so she stayed quiet, the heavy tick of a clock in the corner eating up the minutes of silence between them.

Finally he seemed to have had enough.

'Alexander Shavvon will be here tomorrow. He is the head of the British Service and I am hoping he will allow an end to all that has been uncovered in the Park Street warehouse.'

Such a change in topic befuddled her. One moment lost in the hazy glow of sexual innuendo and the next thrown into a social discourse that could change her future for the better or for the worse.

'Will I meet him?'

'Of course. I am relying on your charms to sway him completely. When he sees you as my wife he will withdraw the claims Kerslake so definitely insists upon and give you full pardon.'

'And if these charms do not work?'

'They will, Aurelia. Believe me, they will.'

At that he stood, scrunching the linen napkin from his lap and throwing it down upon the table. 'Eleven o'clock at the stables. Have

Mrs Simpson ask a lad to show you where they are.'

Then he was gone, striding off down the wide corridors of Atherton, the lord of the manor and the prince of his domain. The room seemed so much emptier without him in it.

Atherton was as beautiful as she thought it would be, the wide open spaces of green leading down to small copses of oak and elm and beech. Medlands had been a large holding, but this ranged as far as the eye could see as Hawkhurst property.

'When the weather is clearer it is possible to see the ocean from here,' Hawk said as he pulled his horse to a stop on one of the grassy knolls. 'We used to swim there in the high summer.'

'You and your brother?'

'My father had a boat made for us that resembled a small scow and we would race up and down the beach, pretending to be pirates.'

'A good childhood, then?'

'Aye, it was that, but not anywhere near long enough.'

Aurelia nodded her head and tipped her

face to the sun, enjoying the warmth and the freedom. 'My mother left of her own accord. A sickness might have been easier to comprehend and recover from.'

'Mrs Simpson told you of the way they died?'

'I asked her.'

'You would have liked them and they would have liked you.'

The compliment was so unexpected she could not help smiling, her horse whickering and fidgety as she pulled on the reins. 'Your mama had fine taste in clothes,' she finally said, indicating the dark blue velvet riding jacket and skirt that she wore.

'She had fine taste in everything,' he returned, grabbing the horse and ordering it still.

It obeyed instantly, but the jag of awareness that had simmered beneath this ride suddenly boiled over, the touch of his fingers against hers laying nonsense to normal rationale, the wind off the embankment lifting her hair. When his fist closed tighter she looked at him and saw on his face exactly what must have been on hers.

The grass was long and a small cliff sheltered them from the wind and from any unexpected prying eyes. Looking around, she had a view all over the valley. Apart from scattered herds of cattle nothing human moved.

'Here?' Her question was whispered, barely audible.

'Yes.' Only that as he dismounted and tied his horse to a bush beside him. Helping her down, he did the same to hers.

'Come.' He did not take her hand, but waited to see that she followed and a moment later they arrived at an overhang where the grass was thicker—a bed amongst the sky, a thin sun struggling through into bands of warmth.

His hand came out to touch the velvet collar at her neck, high and tight, before falling down across her breasts and her stomach.

Then her skirt was flicked up, the breeze against her bottom, only a small layer of lawn to stop him.

He brought her before him facing out and came in from behind, the barrier gone in a single tug and she held her arms backwards, clinging to his solidness as he entered her without a word, the heavy push of him making her arch. Here above the world in the cradle of the wind and with no mind for communion other than that of the body, Aurelia accepted what she had known since the moment of meeting Stephen Hawkhurst on the dusty track of Taylor's Gap.

She had wanted him then and she wanted him now, the dampness of her sex asking for for ever and as he cried out and shuddered she knew a feeling that she had never known before: that of a true belonging.

He held her, his arms around her, still linked by flesh and hands, his voice low against her ear.

'Thank you, my love.'

The tone in his words was such that she could believe that she was his love, not just a wife picked out from jeopardy and married on a whim. Closing her eyes, she savoured the moment, doubts whipped away by the pressure of his body, enveloping her, safety in the fervency of his need.

And then he stepped back, the link between them fallen, his seed spilling down the insides of her legs as he turned her and took her mouth, desperate and urgent, teeth against her lips biting down, the slight pain of sex as tumultuous as the soaring joyous clench of relief, the shared breath between them allowing only the taste of each other.

Ravaged. She hung on as he calmed and held still, head falling against the deep blue velvet of his mother's jacket and her hair covering his face with red.

'It seems I cannot have enough of you.'

'Then it is good that we are married, my lord.'

'You are not upset that we should couple here, outside?'

'In the sun and the wind and above a thousand acres of Atherton land? Nay, it seems more than appropriate.'

He laughed, loud and long, the sound in the wind coming back as an echo, free and jubilant; a Stephen she had not met before, but the one Lillian had spoken of at Woodruff Abbey.

'God, Aurelia. When I first met you at the Gap I should have dragged you back to Atherton immediately and never let you leave.'

'You were about to leap off a cliff, if I recall it rightly, so perhaps you had other thoughts upon your mind.'

'I hope I would not have jumped.' His voice was lower, more serious. 'But war had deadened everything until we kissed and then...' He stopped.

'Then what?'

'You made me feel again.'

Smiling, she raised her hand to his cheek, softly running her fingers into the hair at his temple and watching the gold in his eyes warm to honey.

'Like this?' she asked, her thumb rubbing against his lower lip. 'Or like this?' she added, feeling the line of his neck as the muscles in his throat tensed.

'Like it all, sweetheart.' He seized her fingers and brought them to his lips, his tongue sliding across the skin, leaving trails of cold.

'I love you, Stephen.' In his eyes the flicker of wary green ran into gold, but as she turned to her horse and mounted she knew that it would not be long before he would tell her all the things she wanted to hear.

Aurelia had allowed him her body and her mind in a generous and easy gift of taking. Even now as they turned for home, he thought if he reached for her again and called a halt she would let him slide into the hidden warmth, nothing held back or bargained for. Swearing beneath his breath, he stopped himself from doing just that because on the horizon rain clouds gathered and it was a long ride home.

She was a siren with a heart of gold and the mind of an academic. She was a woman whose ardour matched his and who was not averse to any sharing.

He wished it were night already, all duties to others fulfilled and ten long hours to satisfy himself only with his bride. Yesterday had only been a taste of what he could show her and she was a woman of bounteous charms. He could hardly wait for the moon to rise.

Shavvon was waiting for them on their return and he did not look happy. A group of three other men Stephen recognised leaned against a coach, the horses newly run and breathing hard.

'You are early.'

'Delsarte is dead.'

He heard Aurelia take in a breath and saw Alexander Shavvon glance over at her, the indifference in his eyes changing into something else entirely.

'So this is Aurelia St Harlow?'

'She is Lady Hawkhurst now.'

'You have married her?'

'Indeed.'

Hawk did not expect to hear a quick bark of laughter or to see approval in deep brown eyes.

'To keep her safe?'

'More than that.'

'More?'

'I love her.' There, it was said into the open, the ease of it surprising. He felt Aurelia's hand stiffen on his arm where she held it.

'You realise that there will be a price to pay, Hawk, for such recklessness.'

Staying silent, he listened.

'If you stay for the next two years in the British Service, I will consider any debt discharged.'

Stephen's heart sank at the request. For so long now he had been trying to escape, but if such a duty would keep his wife safe then so be it. When he nodded Shavvon smiled, but Aurelia had stepped forwards, a heavy frown upon her brow.

'No. I will not allow my husband to pay for my mistakes, Mr Shavvon. Instead I will offer you the chance of apprehending more of the same ilk of Delsarte and easily.'

'How?'

'My mother is surrounded by men who

would harm England, men who with only a little persuasion may be tempted to take up the position that has been left empty by the demise of Delsarte. With a small expenditure of energy we might catch them.'

'We?'

'Lord Hawkhurst and myself. They would not trust others and would fall through the cracks of anonymity should you try to do it another way.'

'Go on, I am listening.'

'After this one mission we will be free, Hawkhurst and I. My mama shall be relocated to a part of France she feels safe in and the matter of Kerslake's confidence shall be closed.'

'You have married a python, Hawk, and she suits you exactly.'

When Shavvon held out his hand, indicating a bargain, Stephen allowed the first glimmers of humour to surface.

Aurelia was a woman of the world and she had fought all and sundry for the rights and needs of her family, just as she was now fighting for him. The warmth of loyalty spread out from his heart into the extremes of his body and, for the first time since he could remember, he finally felt he belonged.

'We are staying at the Red Boar in the village and will await you there. We could make for London early tomorrow.'

'Very well.'

As the coach moved down the driveway Aurelia's hand came down upon his arm.

'Did you mean what you said to him, about loving me?' Her eyes were full of hope.

'I love you, sweetheart, and always have done since the very first kiss on Taylor's Gap.'

Her hand came up to her mouth, the dimples in each cheek deep.

'I thought you might say it back to me,' he teased when he saw she was speechless.

'I love you, Stephen, more than life itself.'

'Then let us hope that the task you have set us to do is an easy one and we can be back in London before the week's end.'

'And then it will be finished, this rottenness?'

He lifted her in his arms, sun above them and the vista of Atherton all around. 'Completely,' he whispered as his mouth came down hard.

Epilogue

〰〰〰

They arrived back in England twelve days later having apprehended the riff-raff of Delsarte's minions and dispatched them into the hands of the British Service. They had also taken Sylvienne to a village outside Paris, to be installed in a beautiful old farmhouse Hawk had procured.

Her mother had been full of praise for her new husband and kept whispering that this was exactly the sort of man she would have picked had she been young again. This reconfirmed for Aurelia that Sylvienne had always been an adventurer and the marriage to her academic and timid father had been doomed from the beginning. Their parting was not their daughter's fault after all, and even that small understanding released a guilt that Aurelia had been cursed with.

Braeburn House was quiet as they came up the front steps and she hoped that her father's health had not failed and that the house had run smoothly in the weeks she had been gone. She had written before they had left for Paris, explaining everything, and Hawk had employed a man at the warehouse to deal with business there.

Leonora saw her first and her eyes rounded in delight.

'Lia. Lia. We knew you were coming because Mr Shavvon had come to tell us, but so early...' She threw herself at Aurelia, tears of joy running down her cheeks, but pulling back a little as she saw Stephen beside her.

'Lord Hawkhurst. Welcome to our family.' The words were shyly said and, looking up at her tall and beautiful husband, Aurelia could well see why. There was not one single part of him that looked ordinary.

'Rodney will be here soon and Mr Beauchamp.'

'Mr James Beauchamp? Why?'

'He is not at all as we thought him, Lia,

and he has formed an attachment to Prudence which she heartily returns.'

Such news was so surprising Aurelia could hardly ask the next question. 'How did you come upon him?'

'Rodney brought him around.'

'And Papa? How did he take to all this?'

'He smiles at James as if he knows him. In a way he does, too, because from the drawings of Papa as a young man there is a family likeness.'

The shouts of Harriet and Prudence stopped speech as the twins rushed in. 'We have been watching for you, Lia, from the bedroom.' They curtsied to Lord Hawkhurst before gathering Aurelia to them and Harriet began to speak. 'The warehouse has been run by Mr Steele since you have been gone and he comes in with news of the day each evening.'

'A good choice, then? I should have known you would be able to find a stellar employee.' Aurelia turned to her husband with a smile on her face.

'He hired a nurse for Papa, too, Lia. A real nurse who has been using ways to get Papa to walk more and eat by himself. A doctor comes, too, each day, from the hospital.'

* * *

Later that night Aurelia and Stephen lay together in the Hawkhurst town house, rain against the windows.

'Before you came into my life, everything was difficult.' Aurelia's finger ran across his chest drawing circles as she spoke. 'I thought that I should never know this…this…'

'Bliss?' he supplied and smiled as she looked up at him. Tonight under the candles her eyes glowed with a quiet happiness and her hair lay across him, the silk binding their bodies together. 'Perhaps there is some God-given rule that allows those who have gone through hell to find heaven afterwards?'

'Your uncle Alfred certainly thinks so.'

'I have never seen him as happy as I did at dinner tonight.'

'When we return to Atherton it would be lovely if he could come with us. He does not enjoy the city and…he seems lonely here.'

Hawkhurst swallowed, a sudden thickness obstructing his throat.

'I cannot imagine what would have happened to me if I hadn't found you, Aurelia. You are the only person who has ever truly understood me.'

He rolled across her, enjoying the curves of her body, lifting her hand up to kiss the small ring on her third finger that he had procured for her in Paris.

'This is for ever, my darling, and I promise I will always love you.'

'For ever,' she returned and then her lips came up against his own, sealing the bargain.

* * * * *

A sneaky peek at next month...

HISTORICAL

IGNITE YOUR IMAGINATION, STEP INTO THE PAST...

My wish list for next month's titles...

In stores from 4th October 2013:

- ❑ A Date with Dishonour – Mary Brendan
- ❑ The Master of Stonegrave Hall – Helen Dickson
- ❑ Engagement of Convenience – Georgie Lee
- ❑ Defiant in the Viking's Bed – Joanna Fulford
- ❑ The Adventurer's Bride – June Francis
- ❑ Christmas Cowboy Kisses – Carolyn Davidson, Carol Arens & Lauri Robinson

Available at WHSmith, Tesco, Asda, Eason, Amazon and Apple

Just can't wait?

She's loved and lost — will she ever learn to open her heart again?

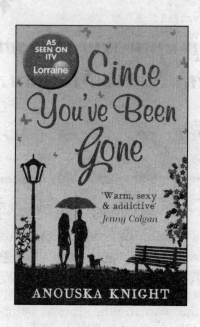

From the winner of ITV Lorraine's Racy Reads, Anouska Knight, comes a heart-warming tale of love, loss and confectionery.

'The perfect summer read – warm, sexy and addictive!'
—Jenny Colgan

For exclusive content visit:
www.millsandboon.co.uk/anouskaknight

Special Offers

Every month we put together collections and longer reads written by your favourite authors.

Here are some of next month's highlights—and don't miss our fabulous discount online!

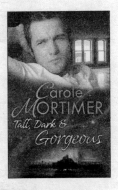

On sale 20th September   **On sale 4th October**   **On sale 4th October**